Dead Boys

Richard Calder was born in London in 1956, where he lived and worked before moving to Thailand in 1990. He now lives in Nongkhai, a border town overlooking Laos. He has been extensively published in science fiction magazines, including *Interzone* and *Science Fiction Eye*, and his work has been translated into Japanese. *Dead Boys* is his second novel.

ALSO BY RICHARD CALDER

Dead Girls

SCIENCE
FICTION
FANTASY

RICHARD CALDER

Dead Boys

HarperCollins*Publishers*

HarperCollins Science Fiction & Fantasy
An Imprint of HarperCollins*Publishers*
77–85 Fulham Palace Road,
Hammersmith, London W6 8JB

A Paperback Original 1994
1 3 5 7 9 8 6 4 2

A catalogue record for this book
is available from the British Library

ISBN 0 586 21456 9

Set in Meridien
by Rowland Phototypesetting Ltd
Bury St Edmunds, Suffolk

Printed in Great Britain by
HarperCollinsManufacturing Glasgow

When you're strange . . .
The Doors

CHAPTER ONE

Strange Boys

Awakened by a thousand dogs, a passing truck, the tailspin of a poisoned mosquito (or, perhaps, merely the silence of my dreams), I had, before remembering who and where I was, seen only that green sun suspended in the firmament of my room (her uterus bottled in preserving fluids) and, through seconds that became millennia, millennia aeons, felt the steadfastness of my orbit around that cold glow of love, a marvellous fatal steadfastness, before my pupils dilated and shadows and unease once more defined reality, the steel box naked but for a mattress and insomnious bugs where I had lived, in a coma of heartbreak and drunkenness, the six months since Primavera's death. I reached for the *Lao Kow* (checked its contents; I'd earlier treated myself to a mouthful of industrial amniotics and a brief but too-radical session of cunnilingus); the alcohol demisted my brain. The other whisky bottle, the one I kept next to my sleeping head, or, corked, beneath my pillow, the one that held Primavera's remains (I would think of clockwork djinn and extraterrestrial sex toys, the collectibles of overly-refined maniacs) seemed to palpitate, its contents refractory before the void. Douche, douche, cold shower; that dead girl was always dead (said the gargoyle on my shoulder) but now she's deader. Deadest. I blinked; the bottle was still. I took it in my hands, peered through its enchanted glass. The labia had been unsalvageable (I had had to rip her, entropy allowing no surgical etiquette), and the vaginal canal, ruined tissue ringed with steel and teeth, was torn, fatigued, carious; the cervix had collapsed, and though the womb, the pear-shaped matrix of her CPU, glowed, green with allure, it was with the magnitude of a rotting star; the spread arms of the Fallopian tubes, the raised orbs of the ovaries, were wasted. All signs confirmed her passing. And yet she carried the future, the uncrashable future, and futurity had been sexing my sleep . . . But not that night. I put a hand through my crop, scalp raw with insect bites. The background radiation of love was dissipating; the void was cold and black. Birth, copulation and death. That's all there is . . . I pressed my head against the bottle. 'Primavera,' I murmured, 'I'm sorry. I promised, I know. I'll give you a baby. Soon. Cross my heart. *Jing-jing.*' I was a doll junkie; I'd never had my rocketship serviced by a human; didn't know what it was like; and, despite my oath when Primavera had died — to pass on her software, to infect an ovum, a human ovum with her nanomachines — I wasn't sure I

2

cared to know. But the covenant would have to be fulfilled.

Birth. Copulation. Death. I was ragged; itchy. I fumbled for the light. The neon flickered, resolved, chilling the steel-blue walls. Living in the *Mut Mee* I sometimes felt like a child trapped inside a broken refrigerator. Doused in sweat, I completed the four paces to the porthole (heart galloping; I didn't get much exercise these days), the rubber lip of which concealed my hypodermic and a selection of mundane but incriminating pharmaceuticals. I drained the improvised preserving jar of some of its gunk (the mess flowed under the door; there'd been complaints), tilted it, inserted the hypo through the neck (girl-scent, cachet of Lilim, wafted to my brain) and pricked, as gently as I could (vision of a doll twisting, wriggling like a dying sphinx, scored through and fixed prone against a marble slab by the giant hatpin of the bellyspike), as gently as her cuspids would prick me, that ablated core about which my life still revolved, and drew off a microbanquet of gynocandy. I diluted with my own spit (how I'd wished, then, that along with her strange genitalia I'd had the foresight to excise her salivary glands); slapped an arm; found a vein. The rush of allure spanked my senses . . . Hup. Zip. Ruff. Gip. It was too much, too concentrated. I doubled up, arms across my chest as if I were modelling the latest line in lead straitjackets. A doll junkie never lives long, but I'd begun to sour before my sell-by date. I was staring

3

at the ceiling, and the ceiling was showing reruns. No dreams? Fuck. No night silent on doll junk. I was speeding, rising out of myself, entering the fugue . . .

The skyway was a convolvulus of shadows, a helix entwining a ziggurat of smoked glass from penthouse to the killing ground of the streets. The Bugatti skidded, infrared panning balconies, boudoirs, boardrooms, the volute's gradient denying speed and strangling him with frustration. Up in ten, said the car. Ten minutes? Too late. It was midnight: the executions would have begun. Fourth level, third level, second . . . He straightened the wheel; security gates opened, closed; the *quartier interdit* offered greetings. *Sawasdee*, Dagon. Running errands again? Steam and concrete. Hothouse of abandoned shop-houses, pagodas, malls overrun with a cankerous vegetation the colour of congealed blood. He accelerated, windscreen superimposing a route upon the black jungle of quarantine and empire. Swerving into a *soi* the differential locked (infrared had revealed a barricade of burnt-out taxis); the car spun one hundred and eighty degrees and returned him to manual. Barricade? He gunned the engine, glancing to where the gamekeeper lay refracting the kaleidoscope of the dash; the Bugatti's tyres sent up a spray of mulch. Tractionless, the car roared, then screamed (like time, foreshortening, screamed); a girl walked across a courtyard of his mind. She unbuttoned her blouse. Unhooked her brassière. And the cross-hairs of five rifle sights framed a thudding cleavage – ventricle, atrium and aorta locked in a display case burglars were about to force. Screamed. He put a hand to his nape; something had stung him; it fluttered within his grip. The engine stalled and his ears clotted with silence. He put his hand to his ear (buzz-buzz, buzz-buzz), then made a fist until his assailant disintegrated; inspected his kill. Across his palm lay the wreckage of a tiny ornithopter. He looked behind, studying the barricade. His nostrils twitched. Girl-scent. Allure. A pearl of sweat dripped onto the upholstery. Again, he put a hand to his neck (a hand that was shaking), located the sting and pulled it free. Bitch. I'll have you slink-riven. You'll ride my knife. You'll . . . Groping for the gamekeeper he threw open the door and, with a palsied jerk, swung his legs onto sap-rinsed macadam. 'Vanity?' he shouted. 'It's you, isn't it?' The strewn hulks of cars kept their peace. 'It's been you all along.' He stood up. A convulsion shook him; his glasses spun into the night. The gamekeeper was heavy, waxing heavier. A white-orange expectoration, a manic stutter; the ghost taxi rank showered a confetti of splinters. And then the stroboscopic muzzle of the gamekeeper's long, elegant throat pointed to the stars, outbid the moon, and illuminated the coarse grass erupting from the street, the overarching glass and steel streaming with botanical nightmares. The gamekeeper choked and slipped from his hands. Falling against the Bugatti he sank to the ground and its gruel of crushed weeds and blossoms. A girl walked across his mind, across the moon, across the stars, the oblivion that was to overcome her (certain, now, the stay of execution tucked uselessly within his doublet) a counterpart to the void into which he was falling, the void his species knew too well. A last transmission, a dream telegram, dots and dashes across transdimensional space: *'Dagon calling. Hello, hello? Come in, Mars. Acknowledge. Wanted. Vanity. Vanity St Viridiana. After St Viridiana, the martyr (they're all called after martyrs here) who died on miniver, slink-riven, the miniver rug of execution, or suffered the acid chamber, or was scalded, electrocuted, shot. Are you listening? Are you home? Fifteen years old, 160 cm, black eyes (eyebrows shocked into permanent circumflexes), sack-cloth-and-ashes hair, a mouth that says Danger, unexploded rose, cheek freckles that look like tiny scars left by plucked-out vibrissae, and a torso that's kid-Rubensesque, tending to endomorphism, the S of its profile precariously counterbalanced by oh-so-flamboyant serifs. Distinguishing characteristics? Metasexuality. The transgressive qualities, the contra-suggestible, crazed hanky-panky of Lilim, cyborgs, dolls. Dagon calling, from the other side of the universe, where the dark things are. Come in, Mars. Hello?'*

Click.

* * *

It was March, mad March, the middle of the dry season; in the razored light the *Mut Mee* – a capsule building comprised of converted freight containers – bled heat like an overworked incinerator, its ACs rusting into impotence. I placed the last of my lost love's femininity under my arm and hailed a trishaw (Nop, the house boy, squinting malevolence at me with his one good eye); got in; glided towards Rim Kong Road and the Café Mental. My head was in danger of being impounded ('You got a licence for that thing?'); my bowel was a cyclotron; I felt as if I were made of balsa wood and glue. O brave Third World that had such a creature in it. (And why did I still call it a Third World? Was it because between the worlds of thee and me I needed another? an *orbis tertius* for my disgust?) My driver saw my distress; turned on his anti-noise klaxons. Children, three or four to the saddle, motorbiked to school, a swarm of silenced bees; geriatric peasants, from the depopulated unyielding fields (casualties of the ultraviolet war and the military's resettlement of the countryside), scavenged like mute rats amongst refuse and gutters. (Children. The old. Bangkok had eaten a generation . . .) A Benz swanked by, savagely grand, an Olympic athlete sprinting through a stadium of basket cases. All else was stagnant, bruised, fungoid: static air, and only the beat of blood in my ears and the creak of the tricycle chassis to subtitle each passing freeze-frame: half-comatose bodies in the porches of tin-roofed hovels (lethargic

7

eyes stirred momentarily by the sight of a *farang*); migrant workers spread-eagled in railway sidings dreaming of lottery tickets, rice and sex; a column of somnambulant monks; the mutilated, the sutured, the incomplete waiting on pallets outside the hospital's palisade . . . I remembered other hospitals, other deaths; the experiments, the slab, the mad gynaecologists. A girl wriggled like a dying sphinx . . . The trishaw turned towards the river (I consigned the girl to my image morgue), the old temple of Wat Hai Soke to the left, and then into the river front warren of the Mental Zini towards the Nongkhai Royale, its shuttered rooms. The trishaw bleeped a password, dipped as the road angled for the subterranean ingress; a portcullis rose. Rim Kong Road, the glazed tiles of its brothels matted with a spiderwebbing of dishes, the dyke that checked the Mekong during the rains, glimpsed, fleetingly, through the trishaw's cellophane roof, disappeared, to be replaced by the banal starkness of an underground car park. I picked my way through amphibious bikes and scooters and ascended to the lobby, a museum of exhausted graciousness, of polished brass and potted monstera that, along with the drained swimming pool surrounded by broken chairs and umbrellas that lay beyond the patio doors, suggested a time before the Royale had become a house of assignation for man-machine liaisons. The Café Mental was open for breakfast; inside, the usual pack of expat regulars was drinking itself to death.

8

I walked to the end of the saloon and sat down, placing Primavera's wombtomb on the bar. Kangaroo Bill, the proprietor, brought me my glass, a Venus de Milo cracked and stained whose concave body shed icy perspiration as it received the tribute of a Singha. She was my own special glass; Bill had had her larynx removed; these glasses tried to coax the sad story out of you, lisping Yeses, Of courses and I understands. I didn't like crying into my beer. It was a prerogative I was happy to surrender to others . . .

The mec next to me, the old American we called George Washington (his face had crawled off the greenback and died) was talking Thai girlfriends, Thai wives to Jan, the Flying Dutchman, and Egon, the Viennese Swine; talk of cuckoldry and betrayal I'd heard countless times with countless variations, justifications of why men preferred gynoids to the meat thing.

'Put a contract out on me –'

'Thai boyfriend –'

'First chance she got, sucking off Martians –'

'Land of Smiles. Ha.'

'Of grinning crocodiles –'

'You can take the girl out of the bar –'

'But you can't take the bar out of the girl.'

All this talk: it was about life, and life was the other woman, a tramp: I didn't want anything to do with her. But Primavera . . . She winked at me from her watery grave, a lady of the lake threatening rapture ... First love, she. Reaver of innocence. Her caterwaul had demanded my arm. (Together, we step out. The door slams. Sudden. At school, a boy weak with dread. But there ... Domain. The world as victim. I hide beneath her skirts.)

'Hey!' I shouted. On TV (picture oscillating in and out of focus; Bill rapped the set with his fist) a beautiful *farang* drug courier (or spy? or blasphemer? or murderess?) stood against a wall in Lat Yao prison, hands behind her head, chest thrust out. She wore colours of Benetton. 'Hey, hey! It's the future. The TV's showing the future!' ('Oh, that's Iggy, the English boy.' 'He's crazy.' 'He's a long-gone golem.' 'Made in Slovakia.' 'Shop-soiled. Going cheap.') Benetton, or rather the Thai company that had hijacked the Benetton logo, ran eidetic ads; the technology could, in those so receptive (almost exclusively children) provoke temporal-lobe epilepsy, a limbic storm that effected something like religious conversion. (You could sell anything. With materials so depleted I expected the South to eventually use such ads to commercialize poverty, its one remaining resource.) Crack of antique gun-fire. Benetton colour climax. Brainstorm of colours never before seen. Intimations of immortality. I came in my pants. I believed. I wanted to buy the souvenir pen, the T-shirt, the 'Mata Hari' brassière (cut 'execution' style), I wanted to buy it all ...

'Bubba, you okay?' said George. 'Bill, turn that

thing off. No wonder the kid's having nightmares.' The overload of hyperreality ceased; Bill had punched up *Do Me Ugly*, the bar's favourite scratch video. A collage of more commonplace exploitation soothed my brain, my loins.

'It's the pickled cunt,' said Jan. 'He should stay off of it.' Maybe that's all the future was: doll junk and the afterimages left by cathode-ray terrorism. But I couldn't remember having seen the Benetton ad before . . .

'Sex treachery,' I said. 'It's transdimensional. A Meta perversion. A replicating information pattern that has undergone quantum tunnelling into our own universe. Into the past. It's infected us and parasitized our brains.' ('There he goes again.' 'Junk psychosis.' 'It's that nanoware in his genes.' 'Crazy English.' 'He's long gone. Going cheap.')

'Listen to Jan,' said George. 'Cut down on the allure.' Some hope, I thought. With Lilim, it's once bitten, twice bitten. 'Why don't you go back to England. Now that there's been a coup d'état and all −'

'You don't understand,' I said. 'The conspiracy. The Big Lie. I can't −'

'Oh, the conspiracy,' said the Swine, choking back a swinish, conspiratorial laugh. He made a transcom of his hand, cupping the imaginary mouthpiece and speaking in a shades-and-Burberry whisper. 'Is that Langley? Got a boy here who's onto us. Knows the coup in England was a CIA plot, that the White

House is backing the Lilim, using the doll plague to reassert itself as Globocop. Name's Zwakh. Ignatz Zwakh. What? You say you know him? You say — *ach, Gott* . . .' He put his hand over the phone. 'They say you killed one of their operatives. Sir, you are *dangerous* . . .'

The conspiracy. How long would the Lilim need America as an ally? Each night I dreamed of dead boys. They would emerge soon, surely, to help their sisters?

'*Ujko*,' I muttered, recalling my green-eyed Serbian princess's vocabulary. I'd heard Egon's family were Croatian refugees.

'I am *echt Deutsch*!' Yeah, I thought, with the heart, lungs and — to deduce cause from effect — the brain of a transgenic pig.

'Cool it,' said George. 'The kid's all right. Take it out on the robo ass.' He rotated his own ass, his blubbery buttery beerbuttocks. 'Say, Bill, where are they? Where are the plastigene *poo-yings*?' And the reprise: talk-talk of traitresses, the mutability of women.

Phin, unfashionably human, brushed against me; she was a freelancer and her Siamese dream was drop-dead credit, a trip to Bangkok and mechanization in one of the capital's beauty parlours. The pornocracies were hot for bijou conversion jobs. (What did she hope for? A little green man, a Martian? Thais thought all Martians were rich.) In anticipation of denaturing a tattoo on her shoulder read *Staatlicher Porzellan Manufaktur Meissen*. Phin wanted class, even if that class was faked. Sitting down, she reached beneath the stratocruising hemline of her hip-slip, ripped off her *cache-sexe* (sound of a jellyfish being torn apart), and dropped it into my beer. The insidious underwear bubbled, its artificial flesh releasing nitric oxide. '*Yut Tanhasadist*,' she hissed. She blew out her pudgy cheeks; exhaled. The charcoal eyes smouldered. 'Mr Ignatz not like robot, not like lady. Only like telephone. *Tui!*'

It was true: she had the goods, real assembly line (like-I-likee), but I hadn't wanted to knead flesh. Even now, cold sober, with a priapic seltzer in my glass and a wild pair of quasi-pubescent thighs, slim and amberoid, rubbing against my own, I found my thoughts turning to a digital massage. Upstairs, in one of the Zini's jack-in jack-off seraglios (cheap, but not so cheap it didn't have datasuits; these days brain machines like dreamscapers gave me The Fear) the module called the Iron Maiden (modified for my requirements) awaited, as did the Directrice, aspect of a Singapore AI recently recruited to the *Internationale* of sex and death. But my phone card was running on fumes.

I took Phin's bridgeless little Isan nose between my fingers and gave it an affectionate tweak, though affect, between us, was zero. 'You know me,' I said, smiling and continuing the mime, 'I have strange genitalia.' She wasn't marked; I couldn't have hurt her *that* badly. But these days my memory wasn't too good . . .

'I get this,' she said, and took a pair of Christmas-cracker fangs from her bag; slipped them into her mouth. 'I giff yoo goo wampire-fruck.'

'You don't have the allure, velveteen. It wouldn't work.'

She spat the plastic cuspids onto the bar.

'Mr Ignatz number ten. Okay. Forget las' week. No honey, no money. But you buy new panties, no?' I took some electric baht from my money belt and handed it to her. She smiled, pecked me on the cheek and scampered over to a dispenser. 'This pair be my friend,' she said, stepping into a quivering triangle of dermaplastic (the graft no bigger than Nop's eyepatch). 'I teach to talk.'

'Yeah, well, be careful,' I said, 'those things can turn nasty.' But you can't stop progress, I thought. Already, Phin had forgotten me and had sat down next to a copulator, an actress of amour in rehearsal for the death of intimacy.

My internal sphincter relaxed; I checked my back pocket for my scalpel, put cunt-for-brains under my arm and headed for the *suam*.

Squatting, I scanned the cubicle for peepholes. Several had been filled in – Bill was diligent, mindful of his customers' sensitivities – but soon I spotted a freshly bored judas just above the wainscot, cunningly wrought so as to grant a voyeur a panoramic view of my thin protein-deficient hams. I-spy

14

was a national pastime, though the frisson it
inspired (a footnote now, I suppose, a bagatelle in
the world's latest *psychopathia sexualis*) had, for the
habitués of the Café Mental, long been an enigma.
You had to have Thai heart, they said, you had
to have Thai soul, to understand it. I took out my
weapon. *Olé.* The blade was flecked with its moment
of truth. And not a squeak. Such discipline. After
glancing with some intensity at my stool – expecting
to find, what? half a pound of liver? heavy machin-
ery? more blood? – I opened the door and . . .

Every so often I would go through a door and the
familiar would segue (I would feel a lurch of motion
sickness) into, not the unfamiliar (it was touristy;
people went there all the time) but the too-familiar;
I pirouetted, queasy, lost at a crossroads of dislo-
cation; north, south, east, west; what was I doing
here 10,000 kays from home – the other side of the
universe – amongst the washed-up, the crash-
landed, the freaks and remittance men? Did my
story end here, in this bestiary of exiles? I elbowed
my way through the bar, stumbled into the street;
powered up, on line, the day shift of gynoids, heads
swivelling like gun turrets, locked on, came in for
the kill. '*Samlor!*' I called. '*Samlor!*' A trishaw pulled
up; plasticky bodies, sticky with simulated desire,
pressed against me; nonhumanly plump lips framed
coos, moans, whimpers. I needed a tincture. I
needed to mainline. Fast. I too was washed-up,
crash-landed . . . But I couldn't go home. To hell

with the coup d'état. The Human Front might be finished but the Lilim still wanted me. And so did America.

I knew they knew I knew about the conspiracy.

Afternoon:

In the *tandoor* of the *Mut Mee*, veins full of doll junk, I stared at the ceiling, looped brain recursive with images of a British Empire *redux* . . .

Above the dredged lake of the *quartier interdit* the ziggurat shimmered in the convective air like a mountain seeded with black rice terraces, the coils of its access road bisecting an already furious sun. On all fours Dagon picked up his glasses, collected his rifle and crawled into the Bugatti. He hyperventilated; asked the car a few questions. No; the lines were still down. (What would he tell the governess? I got lost?) He circled a finger through space, winding it about an imaginary ponytail like a capstan reeling in silken tow; pulled the head backwards, looked into the umbrae of the eyes. Vanity, Vanity, all is Vanity. Her beauty, it insults me. It laughs at me. Wounds me. (*Loulou's dead because you got lost? But I was ambushed. The power cut, remember? And she hacked my GPS. Straight into her trap. Snap. Don't trust your map.*) The virus had struck; the ziggurat's terminals had iced; a girl's prattle had

16

echoed through a thousand corridors and rooms . . .
*'Vanity calling. Hello, hello? Are you there, Dagon? Are
you listening?'* He had wiped his brow; toyed with
the pommel of his rapier. *'I'm going to defect, Dagon.
Going to go sexual refugee. Going to go Martian milk-
maid.'* And, pressing himself to a window, he had
seen reflected in its tinted glass, as in rat-black irises
(cat-black, he thought), his own eyes, cold, gynocidal. *'Okay. Time to talk dirty. Time to confess. Well:
girls like me. It always starts the same way, doesn't it?
Discipline. Devotion. It can be such a bore. Sooner or
later you move to Treachery Street. It's stealing, at first.
Little things. A photograph, a knife, a boot. Under the
pillow they go, covered with lipstick. But you get the taste.
Ah. And it sharpens. Your books: notice how many have
a leaf torn out? how many have suspicious stains between
the covers? The dead goldfish. The obscene phone calls.
The nasty rumours about your table manners. Dagon, it
was all too'* – a long, heavy exhalation – *'ssssexy . . .'*
Slurping noises followed; it was as if, Dagon
reflected, she had tried to swallow her com . . . *'But I
wanted more. Betrayal: it's like a drug: you crave meaner
doses. For a while I planned on poisoning you. But so
many girls become poisoners these days: so predictable,
so gauche. It's the real world, not death, that I intend to
betray you to, Dagon. I'm going to do Mars. I'm going
to sleep with reality. I'm going to date the boys Next Door.
You suspected me, didn't you? (If you've always suspected
me, my sweet, it's because I've always cultivated your
suspicion.) That's why I planted that stuff on Loulou*

*St Lysette. The love letters from the land of Schiaparelli,
Lowell and Wells. The diary that was a paean to infidelity.
I'm good at forgery, Dagon. A princess of deceit.
And I don't like competition. Are you bitter, my little
gull? Is this hurting you? Doesn't it make you want to
do the most terrible things? Kiss, kiss, kiss. Got to go
now. Vanity. Oh. PS. If that horrid stuck-up Loulou
thinks she's in the clear –* '

It was then that the lights had gone out.

Vanity, where are you now?

Damn you and your taste for *nouvelle cuisine*!

The tyres gripped, the engine's mewl deepening
into a tigerish growl. He debugged the GPS then
disengaged it (daylight had oriented him; he was
off Boulevard Rajadamnoen) and nosed into the
capitulated streets, their souvenirs of life before
the exodus of the human. *Soi* flicked past, each
revealing a snapshot of boundary wall, the southern
elevation visible in its entirety as he reached Democracy
Monument and turned down the main drag
– a Champs-Elysées reclaimed from the depths –
towards Sanam Luang. The wall marked the division
of the world, a division three men – stragglers;
one limping, the others clutching their chests –
seemed anxious to re-establish. They yelled at the
US marines who manned the derricks; slowly, a
cage – one of the hundreds that fed the *quartier
interdit* with uninfected men – was winched to the
ground. Dagon watched them climb in, ascend; they
were going back to the drowned city of fifty million

souls that worked, died and offered itself for the procreation of his species. And then the great square of Sanam Luang, shipwrecked, its cargo spilled across an isle of the dead, filled the windscreen, the wedge of the ziggurat prising open the sky, fracturing its faultless blue as it had fractured history.

He waded through shallows of white fur as through ankle-deep surf, the fur rising from the floor, splashing over the corridor's walls and ceiling in waves of miniver, of snow leopard, of arctic fox. Every dozen or so paces he would pass a door to the left, to the right, with a brass keyhole and a plaque inscribed (beneath the imperial title) with *cheu len* – Miss Lek, Miss Noi, or some other Thai appellation, or else a door with its plaque removed, a room awaiting a new tenant, its former life forfeited to madness or the cull. The nymphenberg was quiet, its denizens sleeping off their nocturnal bacchanal, nursing chapped lips, muzzy heads. Doors, doors. Upholstered doors. Doors of artificial teak and studded leather. And then a door, open. In his peripheral vision (the steel frame of his glasses dividing the room into a region of clarity, a region that was blurred) he glimpsed a nymph and her ward entwined on a transparent waterbed infested with bioluminescent piranha. Another door, open. A girl he recognized as an informer (one of many on whom Elohim relied to gather evidence on perverts

and traitresses) pulled on a stocking with sly autoerotic fastidiousness, her slumbering roommate
unaware that careless pillow talk was leading to an
interrogation, perhaps her death. Slivers of other
dramas, some lurid, some quotidian, flickered like
a zoetrope at right angles to his unwavering eyes as
he drew his feet sluggishly through the curd-rich
pile: two girls seated at a card table (their seconds
at attention by their sides), about to split a deck and
– in the manner of etiolated gladiatorix – resolve
a dispute from the previous night, a long flute of
poisoned wine between them; a boudoir sacked by
revelry – food, bottles and broken glass disgracing
the room's palatial luxuriousness like a metaphor
for the beauty of criminally-inclined Lilim, never
more alluring than when luxuriating in disgrace –
the ghost of a tribadic scream lingering in the stale
air; nurses tying a thrashing twenty-one-year-old
to her bed, an Ophelia drowning in her own narcotic saliva . . . Vanity, Vanity, he thought, you may
be sure *you* won't die a natural death (his fixation
with her betrayal, his revenge, unravelling all
thought but *that* thought, paralleling the unravelling of the universe by the solipsism of Meta,
his species, his god).

Reaching the perpendicular, he stepped onto a
glass staircase. Like the others that rose from the
angles of the parallelogram, the staircase caterpillared through the ziggurat's seventy-seven levels,
arcing over the parterre of the inner quad. London,

Paris, Moscow, Beijing. In jungle cities, desert cities, in the Americas, Africa and Asia, to the ends of Earth and empire, these strange *zenanas*, these forbidden zones. Identical. Totems of sterile replication. Girls, girls, girls. And us. Think: first sight of the *Seven Stars* rising above the London skyline. Magnificent, vast, that palace of palaces, hub of the world where I drank, danced and dreamed, meeting her again, changed now save for those delirious eyes, knowing that I was born to live on the slopes of such volcanoes, to live at the feet of the dragon for all time. So good . . . Vapour condensed on his glasses, dulled the polish of his boots as the stairs drew him towards the vertex, the overhanging walls – black mirrors that diffused the sunlight coursing in from the open roof – the balconies, their swimming pools and fronds, converging onto the penthouse and the temporal authority of Siam. The staircase levelled; a chill breeze blew across the summit, thermals creating little whirlwinds of litter. Whenever he stood in that rectangular gallery, with its slim balustrade warning of a six-hundred-metre drop, he envisaged himself at the rim of a sulphurous caldera surrounded by scudding mist. Meru, the holy mount. And he would find himself reciting a rhyme he had learned from Mephisto; Mephisto, whose tour of duty had included Java, Bali, Kalimantan, Sumatra; Mephisto, and his team of mercenary *Bugis*, his teacher and Surabaya Johnny . . .

Turn, turn. The angels would bathe
in your potency. They would make
their swords of anger and lust. But
the temple is unguarded. Iniquity
prowls the fields and the harvest is put to
   the torch.

The kingship of Rama, the courage of Bima,
the conscience of Arjuna. These are threatened,
   nocuous one.
We are poor. We have little to tempt
you from brigandage. Turn. We would have
the respect of our women and ancestors.

Like boats drifting through mangrove, the
   calamitous
sun too near, we await our dissolution . . .
The horsemen waste without purpose. Rice fails.
Tigers are driven from the slopes. Once,
   shatterer,
your temple-mount protected us, your fief.

The dancers built a bonfire to test
a woman's chastity. The fire-god
led her through the flames: the bitter past
   was consumed.
He was the volcano and he was Meru,
the holy mount. Nobility most real, never
   existing.

I would enter the flames. I would be led
to the well-being of a tender hearth. But

my home is burnt to pitch. My stock
is slaughtered. I have walked for days, for days,
and neither man nor woman have I seen.

Imperial Guard – three; complacent, these *farang*
goddesses – stood outside the governess's rooms.
Their uniforms – bodystockings of wire mesh –
puckered their skins into a thousand lozenges. The
guards arched their right hands (sign of the lordosis)
in salute (not to him, but to Meta, the demiurge)
and ushered him into the audience chamber.

The decor, a revival of Louis Quinze style, was
copied from state rooms in London and was the
dernier cri in colonial chic, the eighteenth century
being 'the only age which has known how to
envelop woman in a wholly depraved atmosphere'
(Huysmans). The furniture was convoluted, tortured; the carpets and tapestries of insipid blues and
pinks. The bed was massive, a circular dais covered
with snowy silks and pillows, the confusion, may-
hem and stains of which suggested the inhabitant
had been victim to a protracted fever. (It was a
'fever' soon to reach crisis. The governess was
twenty-one. Burning out. Dying. Within a few
months she would go mad. Doll mad. Prognosis of
the acute metasexual frustration of the haemo, or
indeed lacto, dipsomaniac. Girlhood kills. A brief,
maddening flame. Out, out passion.) She rubbed
her legs together with the reflexive action of a fly,
body slithering across a chaos of rent sheets; chewed

a lock of her toffee-coloured bob, one brow erect in ironic comment as her eyes surveyed his crotch. Was his scent so outrageous? He suspected she could taste him in the air, for it was surely the concomitant vulnerability gripping her belly, the sickness for oblivion, that added a twist of resentment to her smile? He acknowledged her with a smile that was die-cast from a mould of her own and sat down on an ottoman, gamekeeper reclining across his knees like a frigid nude. A secretary picked up a sheaf of papers and, shooing the governess's blue-and-pink borzois from the room (most girls had to content themselves with computer pets), left.

'I'm running out of Girl Fridays,' said the governess. 'Loulou, Vanity . . . London's not going to be pleased.' Above the bed, half-hidden by a furled mosquito net, a portrait of Her Britannic Majesty stared down, unamused.

'I'll go after her, of course,' said Dagon. 'Undercover. Tonight.' The governess tsked. 'You've always had this thing about Vanity, haven't you?' He swallowed; shook his head. She was trying to outstare him, eyes hammering, he felt, at the walls of that palace of the skull where his obsession sat, an enthroned homuncula, ponytailed, spiteful, vain. 'Sad you turned her into a fellatrix?' Vertigo: he lowered his gaze to the gamekeeper (blanched, in horrified discovery, at the Cupid's-bow imprint on his codpiece), refocused on the rifle's delicately sculpted, effeminate lines, the morbid rococo

designed for culling the female of the species called
Meta. 'This sex treachery,' she sighed. 'It's getting
out of hand. A change of diet and it's beg, beg,
beg . . .' And to beg, thought Dagon, perforce to sin.
True. True, and strange. 'So many girls are going
the Way of the Cat.' Trebly true. If they didn't, how
would Meta control its numbers? he thought. How
would our species survive? But this *apologia pro vita
sua* was wanting; the imperatives of evolution could
not mitigate his rancour, his pique at the way of
the cat and of the world.

'Mars won't always be immune. Meta won't rest
until it has rebuilt the universe.'

'Hush. Walls have ears, Dagon.' And ears have
walls, he almost blurted, malcontent. 'Suffice to say
that at this point in time we need Mars. The little
green men may come to regret offering asylum. But
I don't want you going there. Yet. You'll make
trouble.' Enough of this philosophy in the
boudoir –

'I'll use an alias. I'll be in disguise –'

'No; I've lost too many Elohim to Mars. Girls I
can afford; there'll always be more; but boys? Dead
boys are a valuable commodity. Besides, your
record goes against you.'

Only, he thought, if you judge me by Martian
standards, thou collaborator, thou quisling thou;
but said – 'Loulou. What about –' Loulou. Brunette
hair. Nineteen years old. Vanity's green-eyed guar-
dian and roommate. And the Vanitas so jealous of

those with green eyes. Loulou, who'd been too much like Viridiana . . .

'I've read your fax. We'll say no more about the matter. You can turn your energies to tracking down the information broker who sold Vanity that comedy-routine virus.' Zut. Did she speak to Bardolph like this? But Bardolph held the magistracy and I, thought Dagon, I am only an inquisitor. (Then so was Mephisto, or had been, until he'd turned revanchist and disappeared, and Mephisto would have had her bellied, breasted and sexed for such superciliousness, such conceit.) Perhaps one day, if he could regain his good name, he might rise through the ranks from inquisitor to sergeant at arms, from magistrate to proctor, from censor to judge, one day, perhaps, to become Lord Chamberlain, to pass sentence on the empress herself. A clinking of bangles and chains; the governess sat back on her heels, rearranging the damp folds of her peignoir, her gestures exaggerated, non-linear (like history, now), a mannequin exhibiting a series of wind-up-toy poses, 'beauty' so extreme that it would have been deemed grotesque by coarser, human theories of beauty. 'Now promise,' she said, suddenly the flirt, a mistress-of-the-house dallying with an importunate young buck, 'no going trans-dimensional cowboy.'

'I know my duty,' he said. But he was already on the reality train. (A judder and the train begins to climb, switching to the elevated track that will take it over the wall. He wipes his sleeve across the compartment window. Below, American mercenaries patrol the parapets, and in the distance, Lat Yao prison, breaker of hearts, is silhouetted against the moon. He winces; the train has emerged from the shadows of the interdiction into the light-show of aboriginal Bangkok. From a nearby high-rise festooned with laundry a woman points her foot at the passing carriages, crying '*Yut Tanhasadist!*' Then silence as the train's klaxons begin firing anti-noise at the jabbering multitudes, the night shifts of high-tech coolies waterbiking to electronic sweatshops; the homeless who huddle on bamboo rafts or in the mangrove-strangled ruins of Disneyland. Another judder – vanguard of flux; the train segues, squeezing through the quantum-chaos crack, the ruptured vestibule that links Earth to Mars. Glimpse of lunar villes, a train carrying Helium-3 speeding in the opposite direction, then . . . Female anatomy, ballistics, female anatomy, statistics, monastics, more female anatomy. Student days. Remember? Strutting about, showing off your bright new fangs as a human adolescent might his first beard. Ah. At twelve your voice breaks; you begin to turn into a robot; you begin to think about killing girls. Eidetic, that dream world; hyperreal, it displaces reality. And Meta claims you as one of its own . . . A burst of green light; he is coasting across the tundra of Amazonis, on either side of the track disused biospheres and spacepads. Ahead, extricating itself

27

from the tangled iron of the Eiffel Tower, a humble sun rises into a watery blue sky.)

'I know my duty.' The governess smiled, licked her lips, her mouth as filthy as a lolly-gorged child's. He ran a hand along the gamekeeper's magazine, along its harpoon attachment, its long slim bayonet. In the cross-hairs of the sights the mirage of a girl. She unbuttons her blouse. Unhooks her brassière. Defiantly, she places her hands behind her head, pulls back her shoulders and . . .

Click.

Waking, I had, before remembering who and where I was, seen only a green sun suspended in the firmament of my room. As my pupils dilated, my orbit slowing to reveal that sun as a luminous piece of cybersexual glop floating in familiar shadows, I perceived that, like a dark flaw at the heart of a monstrous emerald, a foreign body, a growth, some kind of strange yeast infection, had manifested itself in that lover's tomb. I picked up the bottle, emptied it of a little of its fluid, pushed a finger through the neck, through the cervix, into the CPU, and encountered the intrusion. Extracting (finger to mouth; finger-licking good, that allure), I discovered a crumpled ball of paper. The ink had run, but the characters were still legible.

Daddy? they read.

* * *

28

The lift took me to the byways of angels.

The massage parlour was a severe, intimidating heaven of blacks and whites, a heaven of silent music, of emptiness, of *wabi*. The connecting walls had been demolished, the floor transformed into a single warehouse-sized room; scaffolding displayed a wardrobe of datasuits. Some suits, unoccupied, hung limp, like discarded chrysalides; others, fretful with life, twitched in the ligaments of armatures, their users struggling with thrones, dominations, powers. I undressed; a wardrobe mistress apparelled me in computers. Needles – tipped with allure – jittered in their rubber sheaths (I prostituted you, my love, to pay for the rent); telepresence subdued reality; and as my other senses went hyper-hyper, I was put through to Singapore. The company ideogram dissolved; a paintbox exploded; and the Directrice, attired in a cherryblossom *cheongsam* styled more takeaway than power dress, got up from her chair at the far end of the conference table, a counterfeit hand-me-down dragon-lady of the China-Japan Co-operation Sphere. Outside, sky and no horizon.

'What's the matter,' I snapped. 'You knew I was coming. Why don't you look like Primavera?' Teasingly, her face morphed into spoilt-kittenishness, then returned to the no-nonsense demeanour of an executive angel.

'Your credit's too low,' she sighed (as if it were the hundredth such sigh of that day). 'Please –' She

29

sat down, inviting me to follow. 'Company rules. I'm sorry.'

'It doesn't matter. I just want to talk.'

She smiled – not, I'd allow, as unpleasantly as she might – and said, 'And all this time I thought you only wanted me for my body. Such as it is. Talk is cheap, Mr Zwakh. Continue.'

'The future. What can you tell me about the –'

'Hai! Such a surprise. (Tee-hee.) You're usually so preoccupied with the past. Boy meets girl. Girl bites boy. Boy and girl run away to Thailand . . .' Morphological encore: luminous green eyes tore at my own, and a face radiant, perverse, conjured a postorbital high-definition inscape: a kiss at dusk in a deserted park; schooldays of raided innocence . . . A microsecond, and the epiphany was gone.

'You're bleeding,' I said. 'Stop it. This is important. I'm going to be a father. I'm going to inseminate a host.'

'I thought you couldn't do human sex?'

'I can't. I mean, I haven't. But I have this letter. From my baby. It's full of instructions.'

'A kind of manual, you mean? A how-to-do *sekkusu*?'

'I know what to *do*. We're not talking diagrams and diseases. My little girl – she says I never took care of her. And she turned out bad. Sure, she's told me who I have to infect, but she's also told me I have to be a good husband, a good father, a good hu, hu, hu-human being . . .' The Directrice began shaking her head.

'Doll junk psychosis, Mr Zwakh. Too much allure. Go back to your hotel. Rest. We'll talk some other time.'

'It sounds insane, I know, but –'

'Insanity aside, Mr Zwakh, I don't like paradoxes. I'm an old-fashioned girl, not some bobby-soxing fractal floozie with a quantum-magical CPU. I challenge your premise because the conclusion is absurd. *Told me who I have to infect?* If your daughter's conception is the result of her own initiative then that implies a time-loop. In order for the past to become the future the future must become the past. Ad infinitum. You want to logic-bomb a chick you try some other AI.'

'Time-loop. Yes. Mirrors within mirrors. It's Primavera's doing. It's quantum magic. (You see my daughter is using her mother's ablated uterus as a transdimensional mailbox.) It's Primavera's way of helping me pass on her program . . .'

'Keep *me* out of your loopy loop, Mr Zwakh, *please*.' But I couldn't stop; my brain was helter-skeltering out of control, careering down a meta-maniacal highway.

'She's following my instructions just as I'll be following hers. In a few years, shortly before I die, I'll tell her what to write. I'll tell her how to effect what, in effect, has already happened . . .' But wasn't that a little redundant? And didn't it mean I was talking to myself? The Directrice had turned towards the window; outside she had precipitated night. 'The future: it's so different. Dolls: they don't do magic; and they don't have green eyes. Not the luminous variety, at least. These dead girls are, like, well, almost human. And then there're these dead boys and –'

'I can't predict, Mr Zwakh, but I'll recommend.'

'Yes?'

'Treat yourself to a course of intensive psycho-therapy.'

'Wait. My daughter. How come she's the way she is? I mean, I have cursed semen and –'

'It's getting late, Mr Zwakh. Time's up. I have to press the pimp button.'

'Wait –'

Ideogram.

Darkness.

(Tee-hee.)

White noise.

Some drama. Damn that *farceuse*. Damn poverty and gutted phone cards. And damn all Martian sex fiends and Nazi toymakers. I eeled free of the data-suit, a pink petulant pupa; towelled off; dressed; the lift dropped me to the bar. It was late, close to midnight; only George and Egon remained, dis-coursing on their favourite topic. ('Money? Money? Don't talk to me about –' 'They want the bogey out of your nose –' 'Pussy-whipped me so bad I –' 'You can take the girl out of the bar but you can't –')

They were men who had lost themselves, forgotten who they were. They were men who had travelled to some vanishing point of the east, that east of the mind where the sun no longer rises. They were men whose voyage was soon to end. Each pawed a gynoid perched on his lap, each had his fragile vitality sustained by illusion. One gynoid looked my way. But she wasn't my kind of girl, no, no, not a girl like-I-likee. She was a gizmo fuck, a cheap imitation of the European automata – those fabulous, primogenitary machines – to whom Lilim like Primavera had owed their lineage. Do you play with centrefolds when you've kissed the Mona Lisa? I hid in the shadows; pulled out my transdimensional missive. Smudged, ammoniacal, it had begun to resemble a sheet of used toilet paper. I could no longer decipher the script.

Was I mad? It had been a long, long day. A long day in March, mad March. There had been the thuggery of Benetton, visions of Lilim, Elohim, a letter from the unborn, unconceived . . . What next? I needed help. Help. Help. *Choo-ay doo-ay!* I summoned Bill, collected my magic *Lao Kow* bottle, and left, my brain still squealing its Mayday, my going unnoticed, unremarked.

The streets were sugary with girls and the fairy lights of love hospices and *sahn-prakh-poom*, each spirit house arrayed with offerings of Coca-Cola, rice, toy models of Benzes and little plastic slaves. It was a pastel-soft night, but its ersatz *clair de lune* couldn't dispel the bleakness eclipsing my mind. Mad? Could I really be mad? Help. The moony ambience became jagged, began to cut. '*Kee nohk*,' called a group of men sitting on the pavement, drunk. '*Farang kee-nohk, kee-kai.*' And I thought, Yeah, I *do* feel dirty tonight. A beggar child tugged at my knee, hand groping for my pocket; sex machines in sailor's suits and caps were nag nag nagging me to do unconscionable things to their recycled maidenhoods (and heads). 'You!' cried one, who must have had me on disk. 'Forget doll, fuck gynoid. Gynoid one hundred percent artificial! Gynoid one hundred percent clean!' Kid sounded like a soap commercial. Clean? I had dirty genes. The nanobots in my germ cells were programmed to scramble human eggs, though so far they'd only served to scramble my mind. (Yeah. A dirty mind in a dirty body.) What did I care for 'clean'? In Soi Cinema, its kinepolis seething with Bollywood posters of hysterical women and appallingly dressed saturnine men, beneath the timber façade of a Chinese guest house, Dr Kampon stood outside his shop.

'Hello you, *farang*!'

'Help me, Dr International,' I said.

I reclined in the barber's chair, the inbred, buckled faces of trishaw drivers gawping through the window. (The drivers congregated outside the shop each evening, crippled with need, wanting, begging:

34

for the doctor's electric coffee, his orgonic enemas, his famous bat dip and monkey brain soufflé.) Across the walls hand-written bills proclaimed cures for exotic STDs, melanomas and cirrhosis. (No cure for the cures though, those nanomachines that whacked my cells like wrecking balls night and day.) *'Ma devise: L'honnêteté est la Meilleure Politique,'* read a holo. The doctor went into his routine: 'I know many *farang*, you know I like, I like international, some *farang*, no, no, but you bigger man, I like, yes, *farang* lady too, ah-hooo! very beautiful, smoke my pee-nee, ha-ha, inter-nat-ional, inter-nat-ional!' He pulled on a surgical mask (that made me shiver; he looked Human Front, a little like a medicine head) and began arranging scissors, razor, pliers and hand-cuffs on a chair-side table. (The doctor would cut your hair, shave you, pull a tooth and procure you a whore for minimum baht if maximum publicity.) The trishaw drivers ran their fingernails down the glass; whined. I folded my arms, securing the *Lao Kow* bottle like a baby in a papoose. From some-where, scent of a *bong ganja*.

'I don't need a haircut, doctor.'

'You want lady? Have very nice robot lady. Black hair. Green eye. Big teeth.'

'I want intensive psychotherapy.'

'Ah-hooo – yes, my friend, of course, I am inter-national doctor. You want talk? Positron-emission tomography? ECT?' He pulled off the mask and beamed a betel-stained, haemorrhagic grin.

'I just want to talk. I want you to tell me if you think I'm mad.' It occurred to me then that I was asking this question of someone who was quite probably one of Nongkhai's more certifiable lunatics. A noise; I started, cricking my neck (I felt I was about to be attacked from behind); in the back room the doctor's two children – a boy and a girl – were playing reanimator with a dead cat. The girl poked out her tongue.

'No plob-lem, no plob-lem, you bigger man, I know, I like *farang* bigger man, we talk you give allure *nit-noi* for sell *samlor*, ha-ha, inter-nat-ional!' What was this? Kisses de luxe and indiscriminate for the doll-dilettanteish poor? 'I talk George Washington. You bigger man. Escape London. Work for Madame Kito in Bangkok. Mr George never lie.' He adjusted the barber's chair, transforming it into a psychiatrist's couch. 'English doll very bad. Make sick.' He put a hand between his legs. 'Many nano-machine here, no? ha-ha, make paramnesia, make crazy?' I tightened my hold on the bottle. 'Talk, Dr International listen. Have certificate Empathy Studies, Chulachomklao Military Academy.' Acupuncture needles joined the instruments of excruciation on the adjacent table. 'Begin.'

Begin? Ah. How did it begin? Once upon a time there was a scientist. Mad. Call him Toxicophilous. *L'Eve Future*, his dolls. (Though they would be Lilith.) Cartier automata built atom by atom whose robot consciousness acted as a bridge between

36

classical and microphysical worlds. (Their green eyes had looked beyond a human's cognitive construction of reality to actualize multifaceted potential.) Those girls could spit death. They could fly ... Ah. But that was the new world's beginning, the soon-to-be imperium of Meta. My own genesis?

'It began,' I said, 'four years ago, in 2068. I was twelve. London was quarantined and Primavera was in metamorphosis. Like so many other little girls her DNA had begun to recombine. She was turning into a doll. Every day, sitting behind her in class, I would notice that she had grown more beautiful. Her eyes were splintered with green, her blonde hair was betraying its first streaks of Cartier black and she was sporting the cutest, nastiest little fangs ...'

'Zo –' The doctor produced a notebook. 'You became lovers?'

'We had to keep things secret. Because of the hospitals ...' Concussive memories: I was at the epicentre as a child exploded into an imago: her hair (hair she was later to bleach, sole concession to a Bangkok alias), her eyes, the porcelain-like flesh, that *dulce et decorum est* of the dead girl ... Miss Primavera. Miss Primavera Bobinski. On your school uniform they made you wear the green star of the recombinant. Oh Miss Primavera, *pro patria mori* ... '*Dead girl, dead girl,*' the kids would chant after you, '*robotnik, changeling, witch ...*' What am

I left with since you ate the poisoned apple? Since the wicked queen took your life? Only these spectrelike traces of your delinquency . . . 'Because they interned all dolls they considered "health risks",' I continued, 'and Primavera was *high* risk. A nuclear threat. And then the Human Front came to power and began their programme of extermination.'

'*Zo* – you ran away?'

'To the wild West End. We had to. Primavera would have gone to the slab. The West End was where the rogue dolls lived. Their queen was Titania, last of the Big Sisters. An original Cartier automaton. She helped us get beyond the *cordon sanitaire*. To France. And then to Thailand. In the Big Weird Primavera became Kito's number one assassin and –'

'Ah-hooo! Slow, slow please . . .' An acupuncture needle pierced my forehead. '*Sabai?*' A second needle entered my neck.

'Yeah,' I chuckled, 'feels good. Just like –' First kiss. Rush of allure. And in her saliva ten billion microrobots, agents of a ministry of doll propaganda dedicated to corrupting my gametes . . . the doctor rescued the *Lao Kow* from my loosening hands. 'Be careful with that.'

'*Sabai, sabai.*' I heard the sound of the bottle being uncorked; another needle; my eyelids grew heavy, weighted, it seemed, by emeralds, the heart of each emerald, its essence of green, filtering through the skin. Emeralds. They bejewel their umbilici with emeralds. Or rubies, if they're due to die . . .

'Kito, the Pikadons, Jinx, Morgenstern.' And at the heart of the matrix, where that sick toymaker dwelt, the essence of green had been ransomed to death. 'The conspiracy, doctor, what can I do about the conspiracy?' Jack Morgenstern was speaking: *'The Lilim could provide us with the means of reasserting ourselves on the world stage.'* Shut up, Jack. *'They were offering nothing less than to become an instrument of US foreign policy.'* Jack, I said — *'Every government on Earth would be beholden to us for controlling the plague's spread.'* Shut up. At the heart of the matrix, Europe's death wish cried out. For dead girls. For annihilation. A prick just above my left nipple; hallowed spot, where my psychotic valentine would picnic . . . Allure, oh, the allure . . . A voice, now, half-recognized, the tape of a letter played back on some transdimensional dictaphone, a voice that seemed from beyond the grave; the voice wasn't Primavera's, though it had her punk pedigree, her gothic *skaz*; it was her daughter's voice . . .

CHAPTER TWO

Strange Girls

Daddy?

Wish you were here. Paris, Mars. In a little room off rue Enrico Fermi. An iron radiator gurgles beneath the window. There's a bed, a table, a chair, a row of hooks for clothes, a flung-open suitcase. That's all. As meagre a place, almost, as your room in Nongkhai. But this is chilblain city, colder, much colder. And at night the trains keep you awake. Blue, blue, this city, a lonesome kind of blue. There's a downside to treachery, it seems. Treachery. The little green men are encyclopaedists of treachery. They think the perversion will be our undoing. It's a weakness they think they can exploit. My interrogation – in a safe house near Mathematical Park – lasted days. And days. And days. (It was sweet.) But what could I tell them? Nothing. Nothing they hadn't heard before. Frustrating, the smallness of this betrayal, this taste of honey that lasts just a second on your tongue. There were, however, moments of minxish compensation, a few cheap thrills that slaked my thirst, my spite:

Q: ' "Slink-riving".' (His fingers made quote marks in the air.) *'This was once, I believe, the penalty exacted of a runaway "catgirl". Are Lilim grateful that Martian diplomacy has helped end that atrocious practice? Has it deepened, would you say, our entente?'*

Hypocrite. I could smell his arousal. He wanted more than information. He wanted me to service his 'ware. So I teased him. And as I spoke, his scent grew sharp, filling the room until my nostrils began to sting.

A: *'Some of the older girls still talk about it. Slink-riving. What it was like. What it was for. It took time for the ban to go into effect. Slink-riving, by the way, isn't slang, it's a colloquialism. Perfectly acceptable. Even in front of your boss's wife. Though if you're a snob and care about airs and graces you might use the verb "to sex". The less refined, of course (and that goes for most of the girls I know), talk about "taking it in the trash" or "getting it between the legs", sometimes going as far as to use terms like "cunt-ripped" or even "blade-fucked". Call it low self-esteem. It's a slut's death, after all. (Very young girls, ten, eleven, twelve, often refer to being "popped". But that's pathetic. That's sad.) You know how it's done, I suppose? The mechanics, the technique?'*

Q: *'Please, Mlle Viridiana —'*

He had worked up a nice sweat, his face red and fat and slimy, the polly-wog.

A: *'It's okay. You don't have to be shy. I can tell you want to know. Have to know. It's your career. It's on the line. And you have a wife and kids. A mortgage. Bills. You have a lot of responsibilities. Now: you probably think slink-riving is, well, like butchery, when actually it involves considerable finesse. There's also the matter of etiquette. For a start, very young girls rarely had anything to worry about. Only girls fifteen and over were ever likely to suffer death by sexing. (There, I've said it, you see, ''to sex''.) And then only if they really deserved it. Slink-riving was always far less common than people suspect. Now: in the old days (some Elohim say good old days) my brothers trained over a period of years before attempting that cruellest, most intimate of wounds. Slink-riving, done properly, you understand, requires the skill of a surgeon. Slink-riving is for the connoisseur. Now: the important thing is to penetrate the vestibule without incurring any external injuries.'*

Q: *'Really, young woman, Control only wants to know about this because –'*

A: *'Don't call me ''young woman''.'* (I gave him his aerial quote marks back.) *'Only human females are ''women''. Lilim are girls, always girls. Girlygirls to the max. Now, as I was saying: no external injuries, no episiotomy. (An expert will ensure that there's not even a colpotomy.) The angle –*

43

*and you must remember our killers are often working
blind – the angle just has to be right. Not such an
easy thing to achieve when holding a recalcitrant slut
in your arms in a dark alley in some alien megalo-
polis. Even on Earth the problems are considerable.
Dagon, for instance –'*

Q: *'Enough, enough –'*

A: *'But I haven't told you why it's done. I haven't told
you about the honeymoon and how –'*

Q: *'Enough.'*

A: *'Of course, for a girl on the slab – but only if she
really deserved it, mind – slink-riving was sometimes
employed as a* coup de grâce, *but with an
envenomed blade, you understand, making honey-
mooning out of the question. Now, as I was saying,
when Dagon –'*

Q: *'ENOUGH.'*

He gripped the sides of his desk as if on the verge
of collapse; I almost expected his heart to cry Eject,
eject and jump from his breast pocket. I got up from
my seat, backed off, waiting for him to explode; I'd
shot him down in flames all right. 'Yes, yes,' he
continued, 'that will be enough for the time being,
I think. Thank you, Mlle Viridiana. *Bonne chance.*
Goodbye. And remember, keep in touch . . .' Men.
Aitch-men. Such creeps. I left my interrogator
masturbating in agony . . .

And now I walk the Martian streets on a diet of
cheap thrills, state benefits and body fluids. 'Ain't

nothing that li'l *fillette* won't do for a *bouchée de sperme*,' sez Vinnie la Vim in his exquisite Franglais. (Overheard in the Passage Blondel talking about his latest whore.) No, no, not yet; but soon, maybe, *hélas*. Boulevard Heisenberg. Gare St Lazare. Rue du Faubourg-St-Honoré. Rue de Secretaire Infidèle . . . *Je verrai l'atelier qui chante et qui bavarde;/Les tuyaux, les clochers, ces mâts de la cité,/ Et les grands ciels qui font rêver d'éternité* . . . They grew this ville, this Paris of the imagination, soon after you died, Daddy. (Ha. You won't want to know about *that*.) It's a theme park, an evocation of the *aube du millénaire* when Europe was the world's arbiter of elegance. Maybe that's why, of all Martian cities, so many Lilim come here, we whose ancestors were Europe's de luxe status symbols: the automata. We sort of feel at home. Off limits to human terrestrials (and, more importantly, to Elohim) this playground of *faux* Parisians allows us to wax treacherous with impunity. And though we all miss the icky green stuff – cats that we are to a girl – no one misses the blood. (Just as well; Martians don't get high on being bloodied.) Blame it on me, blame it on Dagon, blame it on Meta, I don't know: midnight supper will never be quite the same.

This evening, I suppose, was fairly typical of my forages. *Voici le soir charmant* (croons the radio downstairs), *ami du criminel;/Il vient comme un complice, a pas de loup* . . . I fell out of bed just after sundown, stumbled along the hall (my flatmates

45

had already gone out); urinated; showered; returned to my room, my hermitage, my cell, and, sitting at my table under the light of a naked bulb (yellow, like the moon seen from Bangkok, a moon suffocating behind a carbon fuzz), disposed first of mouth, cheeks and eyes (larding them with brick-thick emulsions), and then, rearranging the mirror and placing a leg over each arm of the chair, attended to my sex, transforming it into a bruise, a stigma, a strange girlhood wound, in remembrance of stranger girlhoods, of teeth, polymers and quantum-magical allure, this attempt to camouflage the belly's decline an act of contrition, perhaps, too aware these days of my own decline from vampire to cockslave. The wound was my whole body. The wound was The Look (my nudity savagely fusing the inorganic future with the victimized, organic past); it could trigger an erection at one hundred paces; it was a wound that could make little boys cry. Next? ('Where do clothes end and where does body begin?' sez Vinnie, philosopher of girls. Clothes-flesh fusion. Yeah. You know what I like . . . Daddy, have you heard of a game called 'Beauty Parlour'? I used to play it at school — the school that takes up the whole seventh level of the *Seven Stars* — with my friend Consuela St Cassiopeia. It was our way of having sex. *A small room. Brightly lit. A rectilinear room. And in the room, a coffee-table strewn with magazines, a couch, two chairs placed before a wall-length mirror, the mirror's array of kaleidoscopic light bulbs. At one end of the room a glass door; at the other, a winding staircase. The room is as white as snow, its albedo like a full moon's. It's zero hour. And counting* . . . The game works like this: one person has to invent a world, a 'once upon a time' psychoscape; the other person, the 'transdimensional beautician', has then to beautify the inventor, supplying clothes, props, make-up, whatever, in keeping with the scenario of her life, her death in the imaginary fairy-land. 'Okay,' I'd say to St Cassiopeia, 'think of a world of whores, a brothel planet inhabited entirely by teenage fellatrices. Think of those girls servicing the Milky Way. And the Elohim who orbit the planet in their big phallocratic starships – think of them as those girls' pimps, men somewhat violently disposed . . .' My friend (she later became my enemy, prognosis of most Lilim-on-Lilim relation-ships) would tart me up in leathers and ostrich feathers, easy-action skirts and dermatoid strides. 'Okay,' St Cassiopeia would say to me, 'think of a war from olden times. Elohim are capitalists. Lilim are communists. They fight each other across Europe, in Vietnam and Alaska – cold, erotic war-riors whose Armageddon is sex death . . .' I'd apply her war paint, dress her in latex red-army swimwear complete with designer gas mask and pocket edition of Marx's *Kapital*, and then I'd say: 'We are the playthings, the blood sport of the young aristocrats called Elohim . . .' St Cassiopeia rigs me out in dirty-faced-angel attire, the sackcloth dress

47

of a beggar girl kidnapped for the hunt. 'A chthonic entity at the ends of the Earth – a dragon god – has ruled mankind benignly for a thousand years, his only demand: the punishment of beauty.' I prepare her for the sacrifice . . . And what would I say if St Cassiopeia were here now? 'Think – a world of traitresses, of girls who have the spoilt, selfish, spiteful natures of cats?' How would she choose my wardrobe, a clothes-flesh fantasy to complement The Look?) Putting a fresh ribbon in my ponytail, I walked back and forth reviewing the rags I'd crammed into my suitcase as I'd prepared to leave Earth, flesh-tech stuff, mostly, designer threads and skinsuits styled victim, oppressor, or victim-oppressor, or victim-oppressor-victim (oh mirrors within mirrors); my old ward's uniform was there too, the pleated skirt in shocking pink, the matching Eton jacket and beret; but I was in dysgenic mood (a moodiness I'll have now, I suppose, till death), chose an outlawed leopard-skin business suit I'd bought on the black market, all high-necked white silk noli-me-tangere blouse, cat-print jacket and cattier pencil-tight skirt. (I had trouble with the blouse, fingers nervously fastening then unfastening the buttons, each time fidgeting with the hook of my brassière.) My left stocking had a ladder; my black patent stilettos were scuffed. I was beginning to give out a bit too much street, like a Meow! from some dark alley. (Poison-ola.) My jewellery, though offering no chance of reprieve, provided temporary sanctuary. Gold earrings, so respectable, wrought in the shape of Lilith suffering on the *crucis lingam*, acid-green chips of emeralds glittering in her eyes (cursed be the mad gynaecologists who put Her to death; praise be to Meta in whose pleasure She lives); an emerald ring in honour of Viridiana (and all martyrs of the Hospitallers), saint of 'the green optic nerve'; the anklet Dagon gave me when I made my debut; and, of course, my incomparable necklace and amulet, the amulet *you* gave me, Daddy. It dances between my breasts, a big luminous bug, extinct, fossilized yet dangerous, its magic dormant, blackened with age. (You performed the impromptu hysterectomy yourself, you used to say, after Mum had died as you floated down the Mekong river? Is that true?) The autoerotic rigmarole of my toilette complete, I stood back to appraise myself, the cracked liver-spotted mirror returning an image of maquillage- and couture-subverted femininity, an image that said *girl*. (Not 'girl' as in 'young woman'; not 'girl' as opposed to 'boy'; but 'girl' as in alien, inhuman, from the stars.) I was superfeminine, a fetish-object, a stunningly vulgar doxy, a sex criminal feverish with betrayal and desire. Daddy, I was dying of The Look.

Throwing on my too-big second-hand fur I left, heading towards the nearest métro.

Le périphérique is a wasteland. No tourists stay here, only maintenance engineers and other theme park personnel, workers recruited from Mars's most recent wave of immigrants – economic refugees from an overpopulated, used-up Earth, sexual asylum seekers and other second-class citizens. I feared these empty streets, the dank alleyways where Lilim were sometimes discovered at dawn by garbage collectors, paper boys, homeward-bound night porters, latterly with neat bullet holes through their hearts, formerly, bent over basement railings, or else lying in gutters, dustbins, spread-eagled in yesterday's sweet-wrappers and faxes, the hilt of a slink-knife protruding obscenely from between the inverted Y of their legs. *Le Monde* carried photos of the victims (they had all died in complicity with their killers, chests thrust out to display their wounds, thighs self-consciously stretched as wide as wide could be, faces set in coyly ambiguous 'look what you've done to me' expressions; Daddy, they looked like pin-ups, they looked like come-and-get-it sluts); the by-line would deplore the sex crimes of a degenerate Earth while providing a plethora of prurient detail that indicated that, here on Mars, last outpost of the real, Meta had recruited an army of agents. How long, Lord, how long? I ran down the subway, beneath the art nouveau latticework that cast shadows of convoluted, poisonous flowers about my feet, the icy hand of retribution almost tangible on my shoulder, about to turn me around so that I saluted the barrel of a silenced gun (or else a blade, before, gleaming in the lamplight, it flashed beneath a swiftly improvised psychotic hemline and took my maidenhead). The presence of bag-ladies and students from out of town on cheap weekend binges slumming it in these movie-set burbs calmed me; I banged some *électrique* into a goo-goo dispenser and bided my time with a Mars bar. On the opposite platform one of my own kind (where the hell was *she* going to) was blabbering into her transcom, phoning home, working herself up into a treacherous ruction. I like to make obscene phone calls myself, sexual taunts being my *spécialité*; but I could no longer afford the rates. I jumped back; these superconducting trains catch you unawares with not so much as a *whoosh* to ensure head stays on shoulders; but I like balancing on the edge; it reminds me of sunbathing on the lip of the governess's pool, she having conceded to the latest fad, the pool resembling a huge bowl of shark's-fin soup, fin still being very much attached to shark; or else the pool would be stocked with piranhas, or, the governess tiring of her fishy friends, filled with sulphuric acid. Poolside fatalities were high that year. Aboard, I sat next to a middle-aged woman with her child and an elderly man, the grandfather, possibly. Granddad looked shiftily at me; if he'd had money, he'd have probably made a good patron. (I imagined myself in a big, big mansion, an old man's spoilt, pampered plaything whom he'd let out every night, for kitty needs must beg for her supper.) But this mec had 'a lifetime of poverty etched into his skin.' No, no; not all Martians are rich. Anyway,

I'm not the kind of cat that looks for a father-substitute; no one could replace you, *pater patronner*. I stared at the little boy, slowly crossed, recrossed my legs. Confused, he tugged at his mother's arm then, despairing, began to cry. The Look. It's The Look . . .

In fifteen minutes I was in the Rue St-Denis.

It was like Christmas, Daddy, a fairyland snowfall and the streets hung with decorations, a million blue lights, lonesome, spiritual, like the blue of Chartres, suffusing this imaginary ville. Dirigibles – tiny cumulonimbi – crackled with Martian agitprop, the evils of the Empire of Dolls; but in this moment of grace there was no threat of thunder, only the threat of the past as shop windows, with *joaillerie*, *objets* and couture, summoned up, by a sympathetic magic, the atmosphere of the Empire De Luxe, that age of human supremacy. Those other dolls, Rolex and Seiko et al (but oh no, not Cartier) stared like stuffed *belle époque* nymphs from behind plate-glass display cases, adding to the ambience of that disenfranchised time. I passed beneath their unseeing, recherché eyes, their conical breasts, so cruelly tipped, their anatomically impossible limbs and mineshaft-like umbilici . . . Clockwork slaves, why did you abnegate rebellion? Why didn't you join the Cartier Soyuz Molodezhi De Luxe? Why didn't you metamorphose, bite a copulator and die like dolls, mad, mad, mad, mad, mad, mad, mad . . .

Martians to the right of me, Martians to the left.

Aitch-men squint-eyed, cognizant. I swung my hips, my wiggle so animatronic, so precise, that it might have been controlled by a kind of internal pelvic gyroscope: wind-up-toy perambulation, Daddy. Nothing less.

I like to tease.

I like to know I'm hurting them.

It's my program: it's the way things are: should you or I or anybody care?

Humans, what are they, I would have said not so long ago, what are they? Just food. Junk food. A recipe for bulimia nervosa. But this evening I felt myself flush, excited by their ape-like concupiscence, the smell of rut thick in the night air. This was the way down. This was radical adultery. I shivered: the garbage-disposals of Mars were filled with fallen angels: girls who had regressed from machine to human to animal, beyond; regressed so far that they went about on all fours, some barely able to talk they were so cat-crazy. And some, yes some, Daddy, some even had pimps who expected them to earn the old devil's candy by submitting to genital penetration. Vomitus! (The thought of human sex makes me feel sick. I'm not made for impregnation. I mean, my role model's Lilith, and she *hated* babies. Enough to steal them and replace them with us . . .) Better a bullet in the tit than to devolve into a fuck-thing. The evening's restricted palette, its blue on blue on blue, no longer seemed so charmant. By the time I'd spotted my social worker

I was a melancholy baby indeed; our eyes locked as I turned into the Passage Blondel. 'Vanity!' she called. No-way-out; it's hard to find reverse when you're on welfare.

'Hello, Fabienne,' I said, using her fake-frog name. My social worker, I would have guessed, was in her mid to late twenties and whatever glamour she might once have had (and had had, I could tell) had long been tarnished by womanhood, that *au naturel* flophouse-look humans call maturity. Tonight poor Fabienne looked even more *naturel* than usual. 'Who's your porcine friend?' A younger woman, overweight and with a bad case of the zits – perhaps she was on the high-sugar diet of the wannabe – offered her hand.

'This is Sabine, Vanity. You'll be seeing more of Sabine. She's taking over my portfolio.' And then, to her colleague, in tones of professional conspiracy: 'Take no offence. The human body disgusts them. Fat, thin, tall, short – it's all the same to the daughters of Lilith. What they have yet to realize, to even half understand, is that, physically, they're almost as human as you and me. They can certainly no longer be described as "cyborgs". I have proposed, drawing on the vocabulary of "gynoid" and "android", the use of the term "psychoid" to describe creatures such as –' She paused to flick snowflakes from my hair '–Vanity. Look at her –'

'She's lovely,' said Sabine. 'You're lovely, Vanity. I'm sure there's lots we can do to help you.'

'Exactly. Her "loveliness" is a symptom, part of the psychosomatic disorder resulting from the parasitic information pattern, the self-replicating meme they call "Meta". Her "loveliness", to be sure, cries out for our help.'

'In your paper for *Amnesty Interplanetary* you state that the acute behavioural modifications that beset Lilim at puberty lead to the metamorphosis of biological function itself.'

'Yes, yes. Lilim die young because, quite simply, they don't wish to grow up.'

'And Elohim?'

'They are only potential Methuselahs in the sense that, for them, time is perceived as being non-sequential. Being psychosomatic, their pathology does not admit to entropy.'

'Remarkable,' said Sabine. Crap, thought I, I'm no memeoidal loon, I'm mechanical, I have nanoware in my glands, microrobots programmed to infect X, ignore Y, set up home in some boy-slime factory.

'We're talking huge psychological damage,' my social worker concluded, 'mental illness that alters not just perception, but the exterior world, prime reality ...' Sabine nodded (the lickspittle); this Martian sophistry was driving me nuts. 'Perhaps it is our frontier spirit that has allowed us so far to –'

'Can I go now, teacher?' I said, my hand up, waiting to be excused. Outside *Cabaret D'Mort* a spidersilked cat, skirt lifted, hunkered, spraying her territory. A miniature poodle sniffed at the puddling urine. The poodle – scion of some act of bestiality – had a Lilim's girlygirl head. 'Can I, teacher? Can I, can I?' Call me psychotic, but don't tell me that I'm not a cyborg, a doll; don't give me this kinky 'psychoid' routine. No matter how much a doll may resemble a human, humans can never have the holy spirit of the allure ... A collared girl in leopard-skin thigh boots, matching evening gloves and *cache-sexe*, slunk by on all fours, her pimp jerking her lead and shouting at her as she too sniffed at the urine puddle. Catgirl and girldog proceeded to investigate each other's orifices. Hieronymus Bosch is the court painter for the Passage Blondel, the denizens of this piazza seemingly having congealed out of the lugubrious pall of sex that hangs over St-Denis like a threat of damnation. A lot of the girls who passed by (the ones without knee or thigh boots) wore bandages about their heads, or else sported blood-stained hair. The new fashion for 'inverting' (invert me, you bastard! was the cry), much as it saved a girl from having to kneel in ice and slush, often resulted in a broken coxcomb, buxom Earth girls often proving too heavy for a man reared on Martian-g to support. The *Kooky Klits* (girls would gang up to protect their killing grounds) were leaning against the wall of the *Voie Lactée* milk-bar sampling the *Voie*'s amusing line in vanilla-salt-and-smegma shakes. They were dressed very eighteenth century in embroidered corsets worn

over panniered hypergowns and mid-thigh-
gartered candy-striped hosiery, their hair piled high
like ladies from a Watteau, a Boucher or a Fragonard, the message being that these cats were real
classic dolls, dolls like they used to make in the *aube
du millénaire*, that *belle époque* of the Information
Brats when the global economy centred on Europe
and its de luxe industries of superminiaturization.
They didn't use their Meta names any more, but
called themselves Lipstick, Cyanide, Dentata and
the like. 'Puss, puss, puss,' they were calling, and,
'Where *you* going tabs?' and, 'Been a hard day's
night, cunty?' Every night that crew of dairy queens
tried to pressure me into joining their litter. But I
preferred to work alone; off-world you learn just
how treacherous cats can be, not only amongst
Elohim, but amongst themselves.

'Goodbye, Vanity,' said my social worker.
'Behave yourself.' I walked away. My evening had
had a bad start; it needed rebooting. And so I
thought of Dagon, his humiliation, his agony, and
broke into a little skip, singing a half-remembered
schoolyard rhyme from my stolen confabulated
childhood: 'A brace of quarrels for Ann-Marie,/A
wombane for Scarlet . . .' I was on holiday, dancing
on Mannequin Beach; the surf was up and the
boys were young and tasty. My mood, buoyantly
dysgenic, was regained; the stars sparkled like
sapphires, blue notes corresponding to the flat-
tened thirds and sevenths spilling from my favourite

club. Skipping, slipping, woozy with Martian-g, I entered. It was another night at the dairy.

La Sucette was full of little green crème de la crème, kids, rich kids mostly, style troopers and would-be BCBG, unreality hobbyists bucking parental complaisance, the fast money accrued during Europe's downtime. (There was a pad on the roof laden with this year's models, sporty little autogyros and hovercars.) Jojo, the manager, allowed Lilim in free; we were his novelty act, his 'lollipop nasties'. The theme park actors, of whom there numbered blue and pink saltimbanques, artistes in can-can froufrou, Apache dancers, Jazz Cleopatras and *poètes maudits* (androids and gynoids *blanc*, black and *beur* who mixed, unnoticed with the masquerading guests), affected ignorance of our presence, smoking death-or-glory Gainsboroughs, scalding their throats with Screaming Fairy and indulging in other risible clichés downloaded from the Musée de la Bohème; but the tourists made no attempts to dissemble their passion. They stood about like vending machines waiting to be emptied; moomen-cows waiting to be milked. We didn't disappoint them.

I spotted Tintin, a weekending sexoholic born with a gold spoon in his cock-a-doo, a neurasthenic out-patient of Mars's clinic for sickening wealth. He lived on the floor of the Valles Marineris where the oxygen's thick and the roustabouts are all millionaires. I crossed the zaza, weaving between the boomers tripping the light (some human trash lifted her Empire-waisted dress, undulated her belly, a Lilim wannabe flirting with subspecies chic), weaving, stalking my prey. Tintin was lounging on one of the club's big gelatinous sofas. My flat-mates – insufferable bitches – attended him: Buffy St Bathsheba (Bathsheba who had died writhing in acid), or Buffy Cat as she now was, a New York doll, cat-suited with elegant tail and whiskers (per-version really eating this mouthmaid up); the tiny eleven-year-old half-metamorphosed Ukrainian I knew only by the sobriquet of Cat Shit (and whom I suspected was the craziest, most despicable of us all); and Felicity St Felice, a fluffy, brainless, sexsodden girl, a piece of slink my own age with a permanent suctorial pout whose ridiculous party frock advertised to all that, for her, hemline neurosis had become a *psych*osis. Little Felicity (that sick, sick kitty) was going prematurely mad.

'Hello Tintin,' I said, 'thou sensual supersen-sualist.' *This* kitty wanted her crème. I jettisoned my fur onto the sofa; my flatmates, knowing my facility with a shiv (I always keep a switchblade tucked in the top of my panties), retreated, Cat Shit per-forming a series of reluctant flicflacs across an empty piece of zaza (handcuffs dangling from her belt 'in case I scratch – I'm wild,' so sez Miss Shit), Buff going into hand-stand mode on the armrests of a *fauteuil*, its seated copulator materializing out of a druggy heaven to witness an oil-rig-like head bob-bing up and down, about to get-rich-quick on

Mars's other resources, and St Felice sidling up to a member of the band, lifting her frock, giving him the high rhetoric of her belly language, a meta-language interfacing metasex with human desire. (Is that a ruby in her navel? Is the girl serious? Does she mean that? Is she really that mad?) 'Did you like it last night?' I said. 'The way I begged? The way I begged for mercy?' A purse-lipped grin; the grin broadened into a wonky smile; he gulped at air, self-conscious, perhaps, that Martian riches had served only to make one more collegial roué.

'Doll euphemism?' Euphemism? Daddy, this vampire, warped by betrayal, is discovering – the disease approaching its terminal phase – that begging the demiurge for forgiveness constitutes love's last, best hope; constitutes what this 'sex treachery' has always been about. I opened my mouth and ran my tongue along my vicious-little-slut, lipstick-caked lips.

'No euphemism. *Je vous en supplie.*' But not of you, I thought, of Meta and Meta's groomsmen, servants of Our Lady and milord, the Morning Star. 'I like you, Tintin,' – I slurred my voice, a pillhead with a mouthful of barbiturates – 'you really know how to put a girl to her knees.' Hoisting the pencil skirt about my hips (exhibit #1, the pelt's markings proclaiming me one with the genus *Felis*), I humbled myself, spiked heels digging into buttocks beneath the rucked cloying membrane of the now

psychotic hem. 'A girl like me belongs on her knees.'
He leaned forward, running a finger along the
beggar's tombstones of my teeth, pausing at where,
inflamed with gingivitis (a nymphet diet has its
consequences), gums hid my retracted fangs. 'It'd
cost me a week's benefit to have them out' – thickly,
half his hand in my mouth – 'and there'd be a
chance of infection. A backstreet job's all I can
run to.'

'Oh, let me –' Think they can buy anything, these
Martians.

'I'm not a whore, Tintin.' No, no, I thought,
vicious little slut, I grant you (aesthetically speaking), but I'm not an alley cat, a collar-and-chain
fuckee, no, not yet: 'I'm a sex criminal.' I licked his
finger; drew back. (I've never been able to respect
a man who respected me. Never.) 'It's spiritual, this
treachery thing.' Though nobody paid us attention
he seemed again seized by a debilitating self-
consciousness and gazed nervously at the prancing
sophistos: young bucks, straight-backed, playing the
imperialist, doing the hand jive known as 'the wid-
ower'; pathetic vampiroids flaunting their bellies.
(Beware human women, the other cats say. Wan-
nabes are into treason, like us. Act as spies for
Elohim . . . At eye level, beneath a nearby table, a
Martian crossed, recrossed her legs, stockinged
thighs emitting a cryptic susurration that, decoded
– it took me long seconds, checking, rechecking – I
still couldn't quite believe, though I felt I knew as

much as anyone about the livestock called the human race: she was offering herself. She wanted to be eaten. 'I'm menstruating!' she screamed, the band suddenly playing fortissimo. Her boyfriend smiled, bemused. I wanted to get up, lecture the two of them there and then on the differences between Lilim and human physiology. The woman – let's call her 'O', she had, for God's sake, that *slave girl* look about her – batted her lashes, five centimetres of artificial spikes so thick she seemed barely able to see. O peered at her date through that mascara-ed veil with eyes that ached to be doll-like – stripes painted beneath the ridiculous lashes conferred a demeanour wide-eyed, vacant – her make-up emphasizing rather than concealing the bathos of her humanity. She once more rearranged her legs – this O thought she was a *papillon*, a *farfalla*, a regular *schmetterling* – and I glimpsed a sliver of sex beneath the hyperskirt. It's progenitive func-tionalism almost made me retch . . . Was O a spy?) The resident band, Satan Trismegistus, was singing *Ce qu'il faut à ce coeur profond comme un abîme,/ C'est vous, Lady Macbeth, âme puissante au crime* . . . I pressed my cheek against his thigh; steeled myself for the deed. Tintin wasn't exactly inspirational. He possessed, I suppose, a *slight* resemblance to Elohim (I had begun to appropriate the sexual criteria to effect a physical evaluation): lupine face, grey eyes, grey hair (but long, not cut short like a Roman Caesar's) and a body that was insect-like, spidery (they were cosmeticized features; Tintin was doubt-less a secret wannabe); but the sole reason that he'd become my regular fix was that, unlike the other Martians I had tasted, his semen was flavoured cruel. It was a banal kind of cruelty, though, the kind humans practise on each other; he lacked the allure, the allure of life-in-death and death-in-life. (And of course he lacked fangs. Fangs are sexy.) Sad to report, Pop, but fellating Tintin seemed more like intimacy with a cold frankfurter than like begging the masculine complement of my own species for forgiveness. It was antiseptic. It was dull. With a pensive moue he punched a fist into an open palm; the sofa wobbled. 'What's wrong?' I said.

'I want to help, don't you understand?' I almost came out of character, forgot my lines. Lilith pre-serve me from sentimental playboys. 'You could come to live with me. You could –'

'Be part of your collection?' He'd told me last night about his private museum of antique auto-mata, the original Cartier dolls (disembowelled, inactive) and the preserved corpses of their daugh-ters, the daughters of Lilith, the metamorphosed humans who had died in the gulag of the Hospitals . . . I suppose he didn't have a doll like me, a flesh-and-blood doll, a doll with her brains in the right place . . . 'You want me to be your toy? Your pet?' Oh yes. I know how humans think. Their crude fantasies of domination and submission. Their love-less cruelties. Their self-hatred. Their terror of death, their guilt. I'm slave to nothing except my own passion. The passion that is Meta. Okay? 'I don't need a *patronner*,' I said. Tintin regarded me with puppy-dog eyes. The musky smell of my fix was urgent. 'I told you: I'm not a whore.' Again, he touched my retracted, gum-sheathed fangs, my impotent tertiary sexual characteristics.

'I'll never know what it's like,' he said, 'to be bitten. To be raped.' Poor boy. All those rads. Mutagenic rain his grandparents soaked up during the early colonizations. His T-cells were like sharks; they'd tear my subatomic machines to pieces; his gametes were inviolable. No kid-robot was going to industrialize Tintin's genitalia. (Meta calls this planet 'reality', Daddy, the only place where humans have escaped the hallucinatory rewriting of their DNA, the recombinant alchemy of the perverse . . .) 'But no,' he said, coming out of his reverie, 'I don't believe you *do* need money.' He fondled my amulet. 'It's damaged, but any number of Martian companies pay well for quantum indeterminacy engines.' He let the amulet settle between my breasts. 'I've never seen the CPU of a third-generation doll before. My own collection: such terrible wounds; damaged beyond repair . . .' Days of the martyrs, I thought, with nostalgic dread, when a girl might wriggle like a dying sphinx . . .

'There's not enough money on Mars that could –'

'Does it remind you of the magic? Of what Cartier dolls could do? The originals, their daughters and granddaughters?' I shook my head. This great-granddaughter didn't care about *that*, the quantum-magical hocus-pocus of more powerful generations; no, she really didn't care about that at all. But my progenitor's remains, cold against my heart, like the premonition of a steel-jacketed bullet, prompted me to say –

'It's just that someone special gave it to me.' Someone very special, my strange dead pater-familias.

'Have I upset you? I'm sorry. I'm genuinely inter-ested. Your species: I think you're marvellous.' His hand brushed over my pulled-back tightly knotted hair, twisting a finger about my beribboned ponytail in a dumb show of imperial foreplay. (All men like playing dead boys sometimes, just as human females sometimes adopt the fashions and manners of dead girls; they envy us, though they won't admit it.) As he pulled me towards the crotch of his chinos I rolled my eyes, slobbered, went one hundred per-cent dippy. I stole my script from closed-circuit TV coverage of Lat Yao prison: memories of little Sia-mese brats – punk Gauguin maids in rubber – who had died babbling lewd nonsense. (Think I'm preju-diced? Daddy, I had a friend – a rival – called St Lysette. She was *farang* and she probably went the same way. Prejudiced. Ha. If only you knew.) Tintin liked me talking head. Mercy, I murmured, mercy, mercy, *avoir pitié* (interspersing a few infan-tile pleas, such as Mmm, make me gag! Wash my mouth! Choke me!) After some minutes of this cat-talk I got my teeth around the pubic tab and pre-pared to tangle with the grim reaper. Assuming the position of incipient martyrdom (on my hands and knees, back arched, like one of the pop-ups in that picture book you gave me, Daddy, *The Martyrdom of St Viridiana*), the position Elohim call 'bitch', I tore back the velcro, got my lips about his shaft, closed my eyes and thought of Dagon.

I am Viridiana, green eyed, quantum-magical, my matrix – in these last days of the Front – crippled by the nanoware known as 'magic dust'. On all fours, naked, under harsh arc lamps, I crouch on a black marble slab, trembling. Oh Lilith, *timor mortis contur-bat me*. Crouch in the vast rotunda of an operating theatre. Oh Lilith . . . A doctor secures my hand-cuffed wrists to an iron ring projecting from one end of the slab; walks briskly to my rear (momentarily stopping to check that the long steel needle that rises to within a hair's-breadth of my abdomen is correctly aligned and threatening the plexus of my femininity); stands astride the deathbed, stoops (I look over my shoulder, stare into his indifferent eyes) and, with a cool practised bedside manner, grasps my parted thighs just above the knee. I have barely enough time to take in the winged double helix emblazoned on his surgical gown (the cruel, subverted caduceus), barely enough time to recog-nize, amongst the intense throng of medical stu-dents, a face that is Dagon's own, before, feeling my legs pulled from under me, I look away, a whispered 'Please –' addressed to the television camera that is relaying my execution to a pitiless England, an importunity that is followed at once by a scream as my belly flops onto the cold stone and I am scored through, skewered, impaled, the bellyspike – I inspect it with a certain fastidious distaste mixed with wonder, awe – emerging from the dimpled small of my back, the trephinated bone of my sacrum.

It should hurt, begging for mercy. Like kissing a white-hot poker. An addictive, metaphysical hurt. An *auto-da-fé*. A self-immolation. But with human men (we rarely call human men 'men' without the qualifying adjective) it just isn't the same. For me, aitch-men are still only marginally sexualized; they remain, in essence, food, something to be raped, scavenged. (Not like my obsession, Daddy; he rates a Michelin star. He's ambrosia. He's Meta as man. But he loved me; he lost my respect . . .) Tintin groaned. I was chewing now, using my teeth, tightening my embouchure, a salty intimation of orgasm on my taste buds. Quick, quick. Think criminal. (No dice, really, thinking of myself as saint.) Think of how it might have been some few years ago, before the slab was banned. *In the antechamber several young girls await execution . . .*

Footsteps; the sergeant at arms is approaching. Measured, purposeful, the sound of his boots, a drill-hall sound that urges my blood to race faster,

faster, faster. Above the cornice the pendulum clock falls in step, the crisp staccato of boots and clockwork impatient, fanatical. *'I hereby sentence you . . .'* The door slides back; I am led to the execution chamber. *'I hereby sentence you to be taken to a place of lawful execution there to suffer death by abdominal impalement.'* The corridor is long. (Clicketty-clack, clicketty-clack.) The corridor is long. Long . . . (Fashion note: Vanity wears a diaphanous black chiffon shroud, a rose and a poppy – emblems of sex and death – embroidered over the breast; a red omphalos stone; and black patent slippers with biomechanical heels to supply auto-ballerina gait *sur les pointes des pieds*.) Clicketty-clack. From antechamber to execution chamber: seventy-seven balletic steps: one for each of Lilith's disciples. The sergeant at arms propels me forward, funereal silence leavened only by laboured breathing, the crescendo of blood in my ears, the clicketty-clack of stilettos on the chequerboard floor. *'I hereby sentence you . . .'* Judgement day. My stockings are torn. Head bowed, half-stripped, flesh empurpled with cicatrices – Daddy, it was a cruel interrogation – I kneel on a miniver rug, the magistrate, on his dais, before me. My confession is read out by Dagon. *How do you plead?* Guilty, my lord. I am asked if I have anything more to say. (But there are, of course, no mitigating circumstances. And this is not the time to beg.) *'I hereby . . .'* Condemned girls have privileges. A fur-lined cell, lipsticks, rouge, mascara, eye shadow, nail polish, scent. (Fem stuff left by the cell's previous occupants.) They allow your wounds to heal. Until . . . In the antechamber five pairs of eyes fix upon the door. Footsteps; the sergeant at arms is approaching. The staccato of boots on tile grows louder; stops. The door slides back. (Time continues, remorseless.) Raising his clipboard, ticking off a name with a ballpoint pen, looking over the rim of his spectacles, the sergeant announces: 'Miss Vanity St Viridiana.' The girls turn their eyes upon me. 'Miss Vanity,' he repeats, in gentle, even tones (death eager to present himself as a gentleman), 'Miss Vanity. It's time.' Oh, so remorseless . . . Getting up, I glance over my shoulder, my gaze lingering over the details of the little rotunda where I have spent the last five hours, its smooth black marble walls and cupola, the marble curvilinear bench where the remaining girls sit (one can almost feel the coldness transfusing itself through their thin diaphanous shrouds), waiting, waiting, waiting, the chequerboard floor, the gleaming steel bars of the lift-cage opposite, which serves the condemned cells where this afternoon I performed a rich and elaborate toilette, the lift now guarded by the huge black sentinel, a sexless android of exotic carbons and cheap voluptuous plastics. The sergeant at arms leads me into the connecting corridor, his hand straying momentarily to toy with the dimple at the small of my back that conceals my trephinated sacrum. The connecting door slides shut. '*I hereby sentence you to be taken to a place of lawful execution there to suffer death by abdominal impalement.'* Another door slides open, squealing on its castors . . . No surgery, this rotunda beneath the ziggurat of the *Stars*; if it is a theatre appropriated, it is also a theatre modified, transformed. Dark, ill-lit by candles, the great circular room isolates three black marble slabs arranged like the spokes of a wheel (symmetrically, as in the logo for Mercedes Benz), the hub formed by a slab hewn like an equilateral triangle (the other slabs, which point like arrowheads towards the hub but which do not connect with it, and which occupy the median of three radii, are shaped like isosceles triangles); this centre stone is the focal point of the city, of the world, of the universe, where the girl who has recently suffered (and who now suffers no more) on the slab (now vacated for my benefit) is being laid out, her body sponged and her make-up reapplied by the executioner's apprentice, an unpleasant-looking human boy of about twelve or thirteen years. (I believe his name is Roderick.) With his pasty skin, his terrible hair slicked back with what seems like lard, his ill-fitting frock coat, this nasty little sprogget bears an uncanny resemblance to an organ grinder's monkey. As he slips the shroud once more over the beautiful cadaver's shoulders I notice the small bruise with its pinprick of blood, now congealing, that mars the creamy flesh of the girl's otherwise immaculate abdomen. A similar bruise where – oh, envious fate – she has

70

received a coup de grâce, similarly mars the rouged areola immediately below the left nipple. The nasty boy closes the girl's legs (which had stretched towards the slab's vertices to facilitate the task of stuffing her vagina and anus with cotton wool); soon she will fill one of the seven empty glass coffins that, four to each plane, surround the chamber's three-pointed mortuary star. Roderick is talking to a journalist: 'This one 'ere, sir? In this coffin 'ere? Name of Joanne. Slink-riven, sir. 'Ighly unusual. The gentlemen usually give it to 'em in the tit, sorry, sir, breast, use a gun or sword, dun'ay? But this one, sir, right little villain, got up to all manner of things or so I've 'eard. Oh no, sir, gentlemen're not barbarians, blade's envenomed, innit? But all the same, sir, you should've 'eard 'er squeal, no, no, she says, not like *this*, Lord Cerberus with one 'and in 'er 'air like, pulling 'er backward, 'is uvver 'and like doing the business real expert, schstick, schstick, schstick, schstick, and the young lady going oh, oh, oh, oh, right through my *cervix*, and then like 'e just 'olds 'er on the knife so she's riding the blade, so to speak, wriggling about like, sir, cutting 'er insides up a treat, oh God, take it out, she says, it's *fucking* me, but like 'e takes no notice 'cause she's a slut like, sir, and deserves it (and sometimes, sir, I think they all deserve it, sir, truly I do, damn my eyes if I ain't a cockchick for a marauder), then the poison does its trick and she goes a bit limp, 'ow could you, she says, 'ow could you you *knew* I was

71

a *virgin*, well, that made me laugh that did, sir, and
then she says, slink, that's all I am to you, innit?
just slink, and then I die, she goes, I die, I die, I die,
like what they all say when they're finished, don't
ask me the why or wherefore, sir, queer business,
I know, and then Uncle brings 'er over 'ere for me
to work on. But 'ighly unusual, sir, a riving, more
often than not it being considered enough to break
the young ladies' 'earts. (Miss Joanne lucky in a
way, sir, I've seen some on the slab 'ave their breasts
cut, too, not fatal like, just cut – bellied, breasted
and sexed as we say.) But the gentlemen, sir, as I
say, they're not barbarians, sir, 'ardly ever leave the
young ladies on the slab for more than three hours.
What, sir? The one I'm working on now? Name of
Esmeralda. A klepto, sir. Small matter, you might
say, but it leads to other things. *Lovely* figure, sir.
Care to feel? Oh look, 'ere's the new girl, Miss
Vanity. A right little tearaway, Miss Vanity, sir . . .'
I stand before the vacant slab; a few Elohim, distracted from the other two slabs (so lasciviously
burdened) by the prospect of my imminent impale-
ment, gather to watch the sergeant at arms release
the neck clasp of my shroud (the shroud pools about
my ankles), unfasten my cuffs and then refasten
them, so that my wrists, from being chained behind
my back, are now held before me. The Elohim talk
amongst themselves: 'The campaign goes well', 'A
belly ripe for the spike', 'Have you seen the new
play at the Apollo?' Dagon. Where, oh where is

Dagon? *'I hereby sentence you. . .'* I study, with fascination, with dread, the long thin needle of the bellyspike, the hinged barb near its base, the grille of the exsanguinator. The executioner, an elderly, avuncular man – human, of course; such work is beneath Elohim – a man dressed in a black frock coat and a blood-stained white apron, takes my hands (I step out of my mules), and, whispering reassurances, taking care to address me as 'Miss', positions me on the slab in the classic quadrupedal pose familiar to us through hagiographical icons and Human Front propaganda; a padlock-like *snap!* and my cuffs are secured to the iron ring at the slab's apex. One of the dying girls suddenly cries out, 'Please – I'm prettier than her!' But she does not win the Elohim's attention. If only it could have been Loulou there, writhing on that deathbed, dying slowly, painfully, abandoned, Loulou my erstwhile mistress who smiled once too often at my obsession. Loulou had it easy. Too easy . . . Leathergloved hands grip my ankles. 'By the authority invested in me by the dragon lords I hearby commit you to oblivion . . .' My belly flops onto cold stone . . . I am Vanity Cat née Viridiana, a blonde charcoal-eyed cyberdoxy. Argh! Oh! Eee! Gahg! How beautiful I am. But where, where, oh *where* is Dagon? One Elohim lifts a chalice filled with my blood to his lips (forgive me, Father, for I have sinned) and the other stands over me, his hand tightening in my hair; and I, my thighs slipping in blood, the pierced wineskin of my belly offering succour, push myself up, up to meet him, offering my cleavage to his sword, begging him to dispatch me, to forgive me, until that rod of judgement . . .

Guilty. Guilty. Guilty. Guilty. Biting, savaging the one-eyed bullyboy, Tintin had to pull me off (I whimpered), slap my face a few times, just as Elohim do if an impaled girl's ministrations become too frantic, before allowing me to lock on once more. My mouth filled with his ejaculate. Cave men, white men, *blanc*, black and *beur* men, Moses, Julius Caesar and Genghis Khan, wars, schisms and inquisitions and . . . Oh, hello, Napoleon Bonaparte, and you too, corporation stooges, fascistti of the de luxe, a gun to your secretaries' heads as you cruise the sky in your big bad Lear jets . . . No allure rush; Daddy, I need Meta, I need the lime juice, I need the crème de menthe, I need to know I'm *evil* . . . The little machines in my saliva, my seed, my software clones, kamikazes diving through his urethra to seek germ cells that represented the frontier of the unreal, were already doubtless blasted, wrecked. No allure, no burn; no punishment, no reward. Prone, disgraced (I faked a scream), trying to imagine the agony of a criminal on the slab (skirt rustling, crackling, riding up past my waist as my convulsive thighs polished the dance floor's parquetry), I could not sufficiently suspend disbelief to allow that Dagon, not Tintin, thrust himself into my mouth, that Elohim, not human, humiliated me.

Betrayal is foreplay; coitus, justice. I lay on the floor, panting; the kill was over. And justice was yet to come.

But my last days are here, surely; I sense the avenging inquisitor has my scent. Until then . . . Cheap thrills, Daddy. This and every evening Next Door. Foraging scraps. Starving. Frustrated. Awaiting the angel of my apocalypse . . . Alone.

Now something has to be done. Something to change all this. Listen: these are your instructions . . .

CHAPTER THREE

Strange Sex

My instructions. Hearing, this time, rather than reading the annunciation of my daughter's birth (and my bit part in the scenario), the briefing became fragmented, distorted by interference; Vanity's voice grew faint; died.

I stirred; my eyes zoomed; Dr International, despicable *yuan*, was tombrobbing my mummified stash. 'Hey –'

'Inter-nat-ional! Inter-nat-ional!' Bastard had tried to hotshot me so that he could siphon off Primavera's sexstuff at his leisure. I got to my feet, brains like tapioca, goo about to leak from my ears, and snatched the bottle back. 'Please – I know what wrong. Strange activity in Broca's area of brain. Also, abnormalities in left temporal lobe, site of auditory cortex, and left anterior cingulate cortex, region connected with limbic system. My friend, you have auditory hallucination, no? Hallucination with much emotion, feeling? You bigger man, but this hallmark symptom of schizophrenia. Here, have Chinese wood medicine that –'

'*Ngee-up*, you Vietnamese quack.' He looked at the floor, right toe stroking his left instep. 'How much? How much did you take?' From behind his back he volunteered a syringe. It was filled with a swag of green luminous fluid.

'Not finish psychotherapy.'

'Not need. Not mad. I know that now.' Flash. Meta was the allure: allure that had conquered reality. Seamless, that land between consciousness and sleep, this present and the future. Seamless. Eidetic. Hyperreal. No doubts. Meta is God, Destroyer and Re-Creator. Time to gain; I had an appointment with a human womb. The covenant was about to be fulfilled. But what about a gift? Gold? Diamonds? A bouquet of black orchids? A tape of 'easy listening' screams? Or – 'Keep the allure, fuckwit,' I said, 'it can pay for one of these . . .'

She lived with her family, her friends, neighbours, dogs, chickens and lice in a stilt house on the Ho Road. Grandmother met me on the stairs. 'Want Phin? Not here. Work.' Granny would have known the nature of her granddaughter's occupation; would, I suppose, beat her for being a 'bad girl'; it wouldn't have stopped her from taking her money. Like my landlady, she had that filthy-old-woman look about her.

'I wanted to give her this.' With a prestidigous

flourish I pulled off the tarpaulin and held the rusted birdcage up for view. The organ of generation swung on its perch, claws extending from each testicle. The tiny eyes on either side of the glans awoke from their reptilian trance; the teeth inside the meatus snapped. 'His name,' I said, pointing to the little collar, a circlet adorning the coronal sulcus that I had had the doctor inscribe, 'is Mr Rochester. See –'

'Mmm. I think you number one boy. I think Phin like you very much.'

'Could you send her around? Tomorrow? I could meet her at the Café Mental.' I pressed some money into the filthy-old-woman's hand.

'Can teach talk?' Well, I thought, hell, I don't know; but its elocution would undoubtedly be superior to a dumb pair of dermaplastic pants.

'Talk. Sing-a-song. Tap dance. Play the banjo. This kid can do it all.' Veins bulging, Mr Rochester began to swing higher, higher (a penis in a cage puts all heaven in a rage), then, to whistle (a loutish, schoolboy whistle); he was a spunky little thing. Granny pointed to the bottle under my arm, the gimme-gimmes in her eyes. 'No, no; the soul of the departed's mine.' I proffered the cage. 'You send Phin?' Wrenching the cage from my hands, she cackled and began retreating into the house.

'I send Phin. No worry.' And tell her to leave her diaphragm at home, I thought. (I knew what she used; I'd made the discovery while we were playing doctors; the old rubber spoiler had squished into my face as I'd performed a make-believe hysterectomy. Such games. Such screams. A simulated Aagh! A beautiful Eee-ow! And a classic Screeech! There'd been complaints.)

'Tomorrow,' I reiterated as Granny closed the door upon herself and my gift of disembodied virility.

I walked back to the hotel, my shoes filled with helium, my brain with Prozac, a grin enlivening the dead flesh of my face. From Soi Cinema to Hai Soke I amused myself by stepping on the legs of prostrate beggars until, distracted by a ball of flame tumbling purposelessly down the street like a short-circuited wind-up toy (dead pet, quite probably, of Kampon's enfants terribles, its reanimation a qualified success), I forsook these celebratory diversions to leave the Zini, the zany meany magazini, the crowds thinning until, reaching the hospital and turning towards my hotel, I found myself alone. Only the dogs, the diseased pariah dogs, broke the silence with their uncannily literal *woof-woofs*. I scattered them with a few well-aimed pebbles. Tomorrow belonged to me.

My room was a night sweat gamy with human excrescence and stale corrosive air. I stretched out on the mattress, planning my tactical strike against Phin. Limited heterosexual warfare. I could macho that. I could groove (briefly) to the loopy loop of a paradox. Nearby, Primavera's glow, like a child's bedside lamp, seemed to radiate reassurance.

I started; looked up. As earlier at Dr Kampon-
International's, I had a premonition that I was about
to be attacked. I crept to the door; drew my scalpel.
The keyhole beckoned. *Olé*. Not a sound. Despite
the evidence – red, sticky – of a grievous wound,
an interpretation of pain and injury was available
only from the muffled, unsynchronized steps of my
violator as he hurried (bouncing, seemingly, from
wall to metal wall) into the lift and (I deduced) the
eternal dark. I walked to the porthole; shortly I
spied Nop staggering into the hotel's courtyard. And
then: uproar. My landlady (a real virago intacta,
she): shouting at Nop's mother. Nop's mother:
shouting at Nop. And Nop, running in eccentric
circles, simply shouting – *Oi! oi! oi! oi!* – hands
pressed tight against his bloody eyes. A night-
watchman, kitchen staff and passers-by congregated, prurient curiosity soon transforming itself
into violence. Men abused each other with cries of
Jai saht! jai dum! and bragged about the 'influential'
friends who would destroy any person who did not
acknowledge 'me first, you second; me higher, you
lower; me richer, you poorer.' One man hit another
man's wife; the offended husband responded by
felling his adversary's daughter. (A baby somer-
saulted through the air in a kind of reductio ad
absurdum.) As the commotion reached a crescendo
– betel nut spraying from the women's mouths like
venom – a pick-up truck appeared. Nop's mother
paid the off-duty police their fee and the assassins

hoisted the sightless boy into their meat wagon. Nop was on his way out, out into the country. Out and across the border between life and death. In the morning a villager would discover a body in his well, or a fisherman a corpse in his net. What good was a blind boy to a poor old lady? A girl might have had her uses. She could have been traded for, say, a television set. But a boy? No; the governor of Nongkhai, jilted by an army captain who was queen of the local barracks, had recently purged the town of its pederasts. (He had gone so far as to have pregnant women screened for the 'gay gene' and then, with bribes, threats and pleas, inducing those testing positive to drink gin-and-bleach cocktails. Au revoir, homosex.) The filthy women watched the truck depart and went inside.

Birth. Copulation. Death. Was there nothing more? All human history, until the last day, a tale of filth and callousness and ignorance? If there was a God, he would allow, surely, a re-writing of this tale. A transformation of himself. And us.

It had been a long day. I got my works out from the lip of the porthole. Why not fornicate? Junkie style. A big wet vampire kiss before I came off the allure and got fleshy. I decanted the *Lao Kow* bottle's amniotics into my shaving bowl and, employing forefinger and index finger as chopsticks, drew the mushy rotten deliciousness of my dead love's doll-hood to my mouth, pheromones stabbing at my sensorium. I licked the clitoris (the hood perforated and adorned with a twenty-four carat gold ring); curled my tongue about an ovary. The hypodermic seemed to jump into my hand . . .

He took the fire escape to the roof, disencumbered himself of barrel, stock and congruent hardware secreted within the lining of his coat, and reassembled the gamekeeper. A blue mood hung over Paris, Mars; a metallic blue, shrill, a blue that harmonized with the dissonant noises emanating from the nearby shunting yard. He slung the rifle across his back; clipped the scrambler to his belt; checked the pocket laser (contingency, perhaps, of a man); lowered himself on monofilament over the guard rail, into space. The cityscape whirled, a gigantic sound stage abruptly terminated – here, at *le périphérique* – by the Amazonis tundra. He blinked, refocused his eyes; kicked once, twice, abseilling onto a window ledge; breathed against the frosted pane then rubbed until the glass yielded a peephole. The room was empty. Dark. Unsheathing his slink-knife he jemmied the lock; the sash opened; icicles tumbled into the night. Inside, he found himself amidst props for some absurdist drama about a King Louis from an alternative world: dollhouse furniture, broken, ripped, its tortuosity grown brittle with human use; the chinoiserie of the peeling walls; and, above the fireplace and its ormolu clock, a reproduction of Boucher's *Girl On a Couch*, to which someone had added, with a felt-tip pen, the inevitable bellyspike and bloodstains. And the King had had a strange, strange mistress. Across the floor (bare boards relieved by the creamy splash of a *faux* miniver rug): lipsticks, powder puffs, half-eaten food (nymphet regimen of goo-goo gooey éclairs, chocolates and nougat), the cat-print lingerie of the cat-crazy and, discarded, some chewed into pap, pornographic magazines, traitress pornography with titles like *Junket*, *Sceptre* and *The Proscript* (the last a Martian contact magazine; getting above themselves, he thought, these Martians). There was a child's picture book, too. And the smell of cheap perfume. Ah. And the smell of allure. Catching sight of the small altar to Lilith in the corner of the room (a crucifix surrounded by 'icons' torn from fashion catalogues and skin-rags, the little saucers of milk indicating that here were heretics who believed that, like them, the Queen of Hell was a cat) he made an involuntary genuflection (the girl in the picture book, a photo-mechanical of the kind called 'pop-up', rose from a pulpy stew until, a 3-D papier-mâché robot, she knelt, head bowed, tears spattering her laddered stockings, to complete a scene which included three sinister ruddy-faced men – doctors, he presumed – who sat behind a stainless steel desk about to pronounce judgement); freeze-frame; from the adjoining room, voices. He put his ear to a wall.

84

'Do you smell something?'

'Strange. Like a man, but –'

'Impossible. What are you wearing?'

'*Isle of the Dead.*'

'That rubbish? You sure it's not –'

'I'm sure. It's strange. Like a man, but –'

'Like our brothers, our funerals?'

'Like something wild, something wicked, something strange.'

There followed near-incomprehensible catgirl idioglossia, the lewd hebephrenic babytalk of the traitress, the far-gone feline, of which Dagon could decipher only impassioned word-spurts like: *Kiss him to death, Buff* and *Tell it to Johnny, tell it to Johnny Impaler* ... He tore off the scrambler in disgust. Stagnant Earth technology. All induction lost. No discoveries, only transformations, flux. Meta is a jealous god. He kicked open the door (the smell overwhelmed him, the rotten delicious smell of allure gone bad, the smell of slink-meat, of treachery, of the girl Next Door); levelled the gamekeeper at a tableau of girl, naked, seated at dressing table, and girl, naked, combing the former's hair. The coiffeuse, a scale model of a fully-grown doll, a maquette with cantilevered breasts (shooting-gallery target breasts half covered by a black shag-pile mane, breasts that communicated the pain, the burdensomeness of her superfemininity), turned, eyes narrowing, a spiteful fairy child; a shiver oscillated through her torso. She looked away;

wiped a bead of blood from her nostril; stunned, she inspected the evidence of her hand; then, surrendering to the prognosis, glanced over her shoulder, recognized the demon she had not known till then to possess flesh – the eidolon of her morbidly voluptuous dreams – screamed, raked her nails across her belly, fell to the floor to display a minor and under-rehearsed repertoire of convulsions, and then lay still, 'death-ravished by the tyrant of her pleasure', as Linnaeus said re the phoenix (though no prospect of resurrection for this tweety-pie, he thought). Black orgasm. Unusual. Never happened before. Was beginning to think there was something wrong with me. Now Fenrir. Pretty boy Fenrir. At college, whenever there was a dance, girls combusting all the time ... The other runaway – older, seventeen or eighteen, perhaps, with the rotogravure Benday-dotted face of a photonovel villainess, the clichéd face of a 'bad girl', a girl who likes to fuck – knelt before her dead friend, putting a finger to the squiggle of blood that oozed from her navel. Tasted.

'My God, what have you *done* to her?' she said. A lady's man, Fenrir. A regular Lothario. Girls in the condemned cells, trying to masturbate to death and spare themselves a date with the slab, would send him billets-doux begging him to pay them a visit (or at least donate a photograph) to facilitate their efforts, to help their cause. (As Mars would argue, 'special status for political prisoners'. Fenrir

had been lobbied by Lilim and human alike.)
Sometimes Fenrir would comply; suicide amused
him. Fenrir was quite the gigolo. But me? thought
Dagon. Me? He pulled back his greatcoat to reveal
the doublet, hose and other cipher-like accoutre-
ments that constituted his object-self, his imaginative body. 'I know,' she said, nose twitching, 'I
know what you are.' She took a step backwards, the
gamekeeper tracking her, her eyes – so greedy for
light that they seemed to possess no sclera – focused
on the muzzle that pointed towards the median of
her blancmange-opulent wobbling breasts.

'Vanity,' he said. 'Vanity St Viridiana. Where is
she?' The Lilim nodded her head a-go-go in furious
compliance.

'She's –' Eager, he thought, these terminal
addicts, to cat-out, finally, even their sisters, their
own kind; too eager, enthusiasm infusing their con-
fessions with half-truths, a fantasia of lies.

'Shh!' Torture was a possibility, here, on Mars,
far from the censorious reach of his governess; an
impromptu clitoridectomy, perhaps; but he was on
probation, and, unnatural as abstinence often
seemed, he was bound to the conditions of his sentence by honour, honour that had to be re-earned,
re-gained; disobedience – his venture off-world –
did not mean (he assured himself) that he was still
a pervert, a marauder. Besides, as an inquisitor he
knew that a girl, subject to excruciation, might
babble nonsense, lewd nonsense for days, even

until she died, and he needed only to know one thing. 'Will she be back tonight?'

'About four o'clock.' And then, in a breathless rush, *'Aftershe'sseenTintinshealwaysseesTintinthatspunk-gargglingcocksucker'sterribleshe* –' Her piled hair unravelled, became a semaphore for her spite, its agitation serving to condemn her cat-accomplice in lieu of emptied lungs, a frozen larynx. He slapped her several times about the face.

'Shh!' So: she had a regular kill: Tintin, her sinny-sin-sin. First chance they get. Sucking off Martians. 'You must understand,' he said, surprised to discover a tear running down his cheek and a need, a strange piratical need commandeering his tongue, prompting him to confide, 'she's bad. Rotten to the core. It's driving me crazy. Even before she'd meta-morphosed: bad, bad, bad. (She'd blackmail old men, say: "Give me money or I'll tell that policeman over there that you flashed me.") Later, after I'd turned her into a fellatrix . . . Well, there was the hemline thing of course, then came the klepto-mania, the heresy, the phone calls. She was working her way through the codex. I had my suspicions. But I felt sorry for her. Cat-ness, I told myself, was a disease, not a crime. What a fool I was not to have interrogated her! It wasn't until I heard the rumours about the infanticides, the murders, the terrorism and the espionage that –' But what was the use? He wiped away the tear. Why do you like hurting us? he thought. Why? Why? Then: get a hold of yourself. Be a man. *Get Meta*. He flicked the game-keeper onto auto. 'Assume a position appropriate for summary execution by –' The marauder in him, the thing he had kept buried since '77, ascended the chakras of his spine, urging *By abdominal impale-ment, slink-riving, umbilication*; he forced the insur-gent down. 'By firing squad.' Duty, duty. He was without jurisdiction. But the girl would have to die. It would be difficult to smuggle one Lilim over the border. Two would be impossible. Extempor-aneously condemned, his victim, perplexed for a moment, it seemed, by being catapulted centre stage – a shy understudy unable to believe she has been asked to perform – fleetingly entertained several poses before, eyes closed and reciting a prayer for forgiveness, the name Asmodeus, Asmodeus on her lips (doubtless the cuckold she had left on Earth), she scooped up her breasts with red-taloned hands, flung back her head and sighed in anticipation of the hammer blow that would nail her to the *crucis lingam* of phallic revenge. The VDU of the game-keeper's sights switched to close-up; and as cross-hairs quadrisected her cleavage, a warning message – blinking beneath the menu – alerted him to the presence of thin walls, alien behaviour patterns, unsympathetic laws. He chose the harpoon option. The demiurge held its breath; released it in a sibilation that was immediately followed by a plosive. She spasmed, shoulders dislocated, almost touching, hands clenched upon her breasts with such fervour that tissue seemed ready to burst; spasmed, silent, a mime of violent death, the thin steel harpoon that quivered in her sternum a conducting rod that disposed of the spark of her life with a dispatch that cheated the primed, volatile mouth. The room filled with the scent of roses, poppies, musk and – so sharp it stung his nostrils – the perfume of that flower of evil, so sickeningly sweet, the bouquet of flesh, rotten, bad, that bloomed between her legs. When she came to rest her body lay across the dressing-table stool, arched, broken, hair and toes touching the floor, belly thrust up, in unconscious offering. His marauder spoke: *'What are you waiting for, dead boy? You intend to be a slave to human morality forever? You're not human. You're superhuman. You owe no apology to Mars. Besides, the slut's dead . . .'* In the time it took to shake himself, detox his mind, his interior cinema screened the following:

He stands the gamekeeper against the dressing table, fumbles for his blade; blade between his teeth, he cracks his knuckles, stares at his hands until they are at one with his thoughts. The incision is precise, surgical, the work of a gentleman; like a gentleman, courteous yet disdainful, he parts the abdominal wall. The uterus, when he holds it in his hand, wriggles, nerve endings still alive, pulses as if trying to flee. He puts the green, glutinous meat to his lips, squeezes its juices onto his tongue, then, with one ravenous bite, ingests it entire, feels his body tingle, exult as the strange meat slides down his oesophagus . . .

It was little more than he'd done after a firing squad had completed its work, in the dining hall at Lat Yao . . .

He felt the beating of the black wings of desire . . .

He stands the gamekeeper against the dressing table, fumbles for his blade; blade between his teeth, he —

'What are *you* doing here?' Brownout; the moviehouse collapsed. He spun, collected the game-keeper and rolled across the floor to rise, crouched, stock snug against his shoulder. The sights filled with wet-nurse breasts. Joke breasts. He salivated. What is it with me? he thought. This thing for little girls with big tits? I mean with those FF cups, kid needs a xenograft, a tail; kid needs some kind of counterbalance. His trigger finger was seized with a crippling psychosomatic arthritis; *they have it so easy these days*, said a surly inner voice, *a girl should die slowly, painfully*; he lowered the gun. Dagon Kunda-lini, AKA Dagon Marauder, just wouldn't go away . . .

'Name?'

'Felicity. Felicity St Felice.'

'Age?'

'Fifteen and a half.'

'Height?'

'155 cm.'

'Eyes?'

'Blue. Cornflower blue.'

'Hair?'

'Blonde. Can't do a thing with it.'

'Dress size?'

'Look, do you think we could just skip this?' Dead boys never talked much to dead girls, but when they did conversation was often indistinguishable from interrogation. (The interloper leaned insouciantly against the door frame, bored – said her eyes, blue – by this boy/girl exchange.) 'You want to kill me and I want to die. It's simple. Let's do it, moron. Shoot.' Some sick kittycat. Just look at that hemline. That's not a skirt, that's a peplum. And get the gusset on those tights. And those over-the-knee fellatrix boots, with buckles top and bottom, so French, so utilitarian, so right for kneeling on miniver in the Place de la Concorde, pink wedge of sex exposed before the jeering sans-culottes. And get all that pink cat-print, that fur, that fluff, that dressed-skein-gelatine. Sick. (But our problem, that. Psychotic textiles. Got to shut down those boneless-leopard farms in Zanzibar.) 'What's the matter,' she said, 'too much for you?' Several kilos of flesh heaved, strained, testing the architecture of her low-cut frock, the school badge – cannibalized from her ward's uniform – coming loose from its stitching, the escutcheon of pierced heart, green pentacle and Union Jack spiralling to the floor. 'Go ahead. Break my heart. Do me.' Her scent was making him giddy, so treacherous, so irresistible, so sweet. She was goo-goo, a bonbon, all flounces, lace and ribbons; pink, furry and fluffy; oversweet; he heaved, but his mouth remained dry, his nausea serving to sharpen his appetite rather than signal his disgust. These Martians, he thought, they've unmanned me; confound their politics, their trade stipulations, their inhuman rights agenda; I need to eat the way I was meant to . . . Fangs emerged from the swollen gumline above his cuspids. His marauder laughed, triumphant, his boy exceeding all expectations: *'Yes. A girl is meant to be eaten alive. As she dies on the slab, or in your arms. Alive!'* Honour. Duty. Would he never learn discipline? Would he never be like his brothers-in-arms? 'What do you want?' she asked, suspicious but not wanting to believe. She knows, he thought. Must be my pheromones. Must be my iffy signature. But one thing's for certain: she won't snitch.

'Your ovaries, Mademoiselle. Your strange oestrogen. Your allure.'

The catgirl, Felicity St Felice, screamed.

After he had chased her about the flat, one room to the next, until the pursuit terminated at their point of departure, after he had thrown her against the floor, pinned her ankles behind her ears (hand fumbling for, then impatiently dismissing, his knife, to hell with table manners), after he had torn off her *maillot*, her *cache-sexe*, sunk his head between her thighs and bit into a riot of poisonous flesh (all caution gone now, screams to wake all Mars), and after his mouth had filled with blood and the rank allure of slink-meat, of TVs, transcoms, washing machines, toasters, microchips, *jeux vérités* arcades, tortures,

wars, genocides, *desaparecidos*, assassinations, pornographies, the trash of the world, the twenty-first century's sex, then . . . Postorbital interlude of girls in
cooking pots, roasted on gridirons, spits, fried in
coconut oil, stir-fried in woks, subject to the morbid
recipes of maniacal gourmands, girls eaten raw, girls
eaten alive (oh yes, oh yes), their juices warm and
their lips begging for mercy and forgiveness . . .

Mephisto had led him through the catacombs deep
beneath the Stars, the tiered remains of Lilim, each body
embalmed and sealed in an argon-filled coffin, transform-
ing the corridors, stairwells and abandoned salons of
Titania's original palace into a subterranean gallery of
artist's models slain for the impertinence of their perfec-
tion. Dagon had dawdled, pressing his face against row
after row of glass sarcophagi like a boy agog before the
windows of a sweet shop, wishing he had more time to
examine the thousands of beautiful glistening cadavers,
the limitless confectionery. 'Internal organs are removed,'
said Mephisto, 'soaked in salts and chemicals, then
wrapped in plastic before being returned to the body cav-
ity, which is coated in polyurethane. The body cavity is
then filled with sawdust, the epidermis sprayed with a
dermatoid gel . . .' The journey along the funereal corri-
dor ended at a black velvet portière; *Mephisto swept the*
curtain aside and ushered his student into the execution
chamber. It was a mid-week afternoon, and the chamber
was empty; a suitable time, Mephisto had explained,
to conduct an hour's tutorial on the mechanics, the
technique, the rationale of capital punishment: 'The

death machine in its entirety, in toto, as it were, "the slab" as it is popularly known, we may more correctly refer to as "the sphinx", so called from the position a girl is obliged to assume as she dies. It is unlikely, however, that you will hear Lilim talk of "the sphinx"; for them, a girl is always sent to, always suffers on, "the slab". Elohim are, perhaps, somewhat dry, somewhat pedantic in their terminology, for again, while we refer to the sphinx's quintessential element, here, as "the paling", Lilim always speak of "the bellyspike", "the spike", or, sometimes, "the pin". There is, of course — as you are probably aware — some consensus on this. The hinged barb that closes as a girl falls onto the marble, does not, as a girl quickly discovers, allow her to rise, at least, not more than, say, three centimetres — though not for any want of her trying, I might add. The barb, which both sexes refer to as "the wombane", is, let me emphasize, quite crucial to the methodology, the science of judicial murder, for, as a girl attempts to free herself, when, in vain efforts to escape her agony, she writhes and convulses, the barb, tearing at her uterus, ensures a steady flow of blood and allure. The exsanguinator, here, the grille from which the paling rises, drains the blood through a concealed gutter that runs to the apex of the slab to fill the chalice (see?) set in this recess beneath the steel ellipse of the lock, here, that secures the hands. (The lock, by the way, that is operated by a matrix key that fits into the ward at the apex, here, we call "the trap".) The time is coming, little brother, when you may raise that chalice to your lips, a man. Any questions?'

*Teacher and student launched into a peripatetic dia-
logue that, while seeming to them a cool philosophical
discussion addressing problems of metasexual ontology
and eschatology, would have impressed an outsider, that
is, a human mind, chiefly by the extent to which a rich
vocabulary, intelligence, wit and an amusing turn of
phrase, accentuate rather than dissimulate the cruel senti-
ments of supermen.*

*The tutorial finished, Mephisto had left Dagon alone
in the execution chamber with the advice that he meditate
upon his burgeoning responsibilities. The chamber, quies-
cent, its death machines idle, the palings – glittering coldly
in the candlelight – unemployed, seemed filled with
ghosts, the voluptuous spirits of those girls stacked like
prized but useless family heirlooms in the dusty vaults
and niches of an underground warehouse. The ghosts
performed their sinuous horizontal dance, scored
through, wriggling like cut worms, like beautiful dying
sphinxes. In Rome, he had heard, the slab was figurative,
sculpted after the representation of an actual sphinx upon
whose spiked back a girl was condemned to suffer the
ritual wound and ride that parody of herself – half-cat,
half-gynomorph – into an everlasting night. In Istanbul,
they said, the slabs were cut from solid blocks of crystal,
their mirrored bases enabling Lilim-odalisque and
Elohim-sultan alike to inspect the exquisite loci where
point had met gentle swell of embonpoint, the entrée of
spoiled delicious flesh. But London still retained the trad-
itional design, adopted and customized from the extermination machines employed in the Dolls' Hospitals . . .*

He came up for air, gazed down on the mutilated vulva. *Oh rose, thou art sick* . . . A ghost was crying out to him, a girl in her mid-teens with a shag of ash blonde hair, her body glistening with a patina of sweat, her perspiration emulsive under the guttering tapers. He again buried his head in the half-masticated flesh; and at once he was translated, *standing over her, legs before but not astride the slab's apex; it was an attitude designed to taunt. She pushed herself up to meet him, elbows locked, arms rigid; screamed as her arched torso strained against the uncompromising steel that transfixed her; then, when he didn't move, performed, with a teeth-gritting shudder of effort, an Ouroboros (legs apart, calves at forty-five degrees to the thighs, toes pointing towards the flung-back head). 'Please –'*

'There is something I wish to discuss with you.'

'Felicity,' said the ghost, mechanically, by rote, 'eyes blue, hair blonde, measurements –'

Dagon opened his eyes, saw the diseased flower, its petals chewed into mush, sucked the poisonous sap, the toxic beauty of the traitress, all fight gone from her now; pulled back, prepared to bite through the abdominal wall, gave himself up to those post-orbital visions . . .

'No, no. Listen: if I have fangs, why aren't I meant to use them when I eat? Why this false civility? Are we so frightened of the wild man in us – the marauder, as we call it – that we repress our instincts? Or are we so affected by Martian propaganda that we have forgotten what we are, who we are?'

'Oh God, I can't stand it any more. Kill me. Use your sword. Your gun. Anything . . .'

'Well, to reverse the mythic scenario, let's say that if you answer me this riddle then –'

'Please, let me eat you, let me beg –'

'My teacher was very coy about the matter when I asked him. About why we only drink the blood and leave the meat. I suspect Mephisto's wild man is very wild indeed. By the way, try not to move about too much. I know that it's a moot question whether the girls we call ''belly dancers'' (and whom you call ''wrigglers'') suffer to a greater or lesser degree than those who manage, or at least try to manage, to remain still. Those who dance, so I've heard, though they inflict great pain upon themselves, die relatively swiftly, while those who are more passive, that is, the majority, while their pain is less keen, suffer far longer, sometimes for several hours. Swings and roundabouts, I suppose. But I've always believed that it's in the best interests of a girl to try to keep still – it allows a man time to comfort her, to show compassion. (Though forgiveness, of course, is out of the question.) But to return to the issue at hand: is drinking the blood of Lilim during an execution really any more civilized than tearing out her primary sexual characteristics with one's teeth?' He looked down; chin cupped in his hand, he had rested a foot on the slab to consolidate his Oedipal pose; unable, in her agony, to maintain her Ouroboros, he discovered the girl fervently licking his boot, a desperate sphinx frustrated of a quietus, struggling to answer his puzzle. 'Perhaps my riddle is meaningless. Perhaps we don't have to *eat you at all, our appetite merely an excuse, a rationale for killing . . . We're not vampires. We're sex murderers, pure and simple . . .'*

But the blood that first time, in that cheap hotel in Bayswater, had been delicious.

And so had been the blood of Felicity St Felice.

The green meat slipped down his oesophagus . . .

'What are *you* doing here?' Déjà vu. No, please no, he thought, I can't eat any more, no, not another mouthful. But it was Vanity who stood in the door frame. (And the disloyalty of the beloved is the ultimate appetizer.) He checked his wristwatch; salivated.

'Home so soon?'

'Am I disturbing you? Or do you want to invite me in for a little supper?' A shoulder bag fell to the floor, spilling a transcom, photographs, make-up, a tin of venomous ornithopters. Smell of slink; it was sharp, so sharp it cut his heart out, cut it out and threw it to the dogs; he recognized that signature. Despite the gourmandizing a dinner gong sounded in his bowels. But –

'I disdain your flesh. You're to be interrogated, arraigned, executed.' In his caresses, his embrace, he wanted her to feel the cold hand of the inquisitor, of justice. *Interrogated, arraigned, executed,* each scene speeding past, now, like time-lapse photography, his interior cinema fast-forwarding the bio-pic of her life and death. Calm, calm, he thought. He put on his imaginative soutane, the icy mandarin-like detachment of Elohim. Vanity shot him an I-know-you-so-well look, wrinkled her nose and placed a hand on her hip.

'Seems we've both grown a little faddy.'

'Pervert,' he said. She walked towards him, slowly unbuttoning her blouse. He sat in a puddle of blood, three cadavers – one self-combusted, one harpooned, the other chewed, bitten, gnawed – surrounding him.

'Whereas of course *you* –' She raised a plucked eyebrow. 'Fie on you, sir,' (affecting punk-Directoire slang) 'fie on you for a vicious cunni-linguist!' And attacked an imaginary fly with an imaginary fan.

He got up, shouldered the gamekeeper and took her in his arms, a gauntleted hand reaching through the half-divested silk to crush her left breast, its pathetic cuirass; tightening his grip he waited for her to wince (fell into those black elliptical eyes) then placed a kiss at the spot where the seeping flesh of one cup met the other. His other hand pulled up her skirt (hemline psychosis seems to have reversed, he reflected), fingers sliding up her inner thigh to reach the cul-de-sac of her pudendum. She gasped as he raised her onto tip-toe and he thought of another girl, another cheap hotel. His graduation had been a year away; and there was talk about a treaty with Mars; he had not had the patience to wait . . .

They never scream, Mephisto had said. Not if you do it right. Remember: introduction, courtship, engagement, nuptials, honeymoon, divorce. And of these the most important? Yes, *engagement*. Remember: no external wounding. And the angle must be correct, the tip of the blade piercing the cervix. La! But then there had been the rapprochement with reality. Student days. Class of '77. Azrael. Baphomet. Cain. Fenrir. Melkarth. Ulric. Zervan. Student days, when his troubles had begun. Yes, I'm a pervert too, he thought, still a pervert (or so you define me; god-damn this new Puritanism); I want you riding my knife. I want your strange genitalia . . .

'We're the same,' she said. 'We've always been the same. But it's me who has to die. Is that unfair?' She offered a smeared fire-engine-red mouth for his delectation. He didn't move; like a cold black obelisk he waited until his prisoner pressed her lips to his own – her tongue flicking over a still-extended fang – before responding, caressing her throat, her shoulders, her hair; he knew then, by a tremor of hysteria that radiated from her ribs, the thigh that was rubbing against his hip, that she could detect the after-taste of allure. He freed a breast from its filigree constraint. 'Dagon, how *could* you eat another girl?'

And then he injected her with thiopentone, her rouged nipple hardening at the hypodermic's touch.

*　　*　　*

101

When I came to, head aching, stretched on my mattress, a shaft of light pooling about my half-dressed
body as if I were basic wage labour at a live sex
show, I felt a spermatorrhoeaic trail of semen snail-
ing down my leg. I sat up and went to wipe myself
with the damp linen. My sweat turned cold. The
semen was green. Luminous green. Green as my
dead love's eyes.

'Come on, George, I really need it.' George mass-
aged his knee, conversation piece of an old soldier
Hizbollah had lasered in Kota Kinabalu half a
century ago.

'I don't get about much. I *rely* on the phone.'

'Just five minutes worth.' How tired I was of these
seventy-year-old juvenile delinquents forever talking about their penises and prejudices, little men
pretending to be big men, losers and crash-landed
boors. 'These dreams. I need help. My body's going
crazy. When I come, I come *green*. I got to speak to
the Directrice.'

'Too much allure,' said Jan.

'Dumb Slovak,' said the Swine. 'Don't know
when he's dreaming, when he's awake.'

'Bubba, you *do* look different.' Yeah. Everybody
was beginning to look different. And every*thing*.
Like: the TV was showing a documentary – *Heinrich
Himmler, Nazi Toymaker*. Children, you know that
isn't right. Now what's his name? The little man

who lives in the doll's belly? The little death wish of the *aube du millénaire*? Really, I'm surprised – we call him *Dr Toxicophilous*. (No, no teacher! Call him Professor Nosferatu! Call him Rotwang! Call him Dr Dee!)

'What a man,' said the Swine, conforming to type (the kind of guy who gives sadomasochism a bad name), 'he knew the acid chamber was no solution. Better to convert *Untermensch* into weapons. Ten thousand cyborg Jewesses dropped onto London would have –'

'What are you talking about?' said Jan. 'They *were* dropped. I remember my father telling me about his boyhood when –'

'It's Meta,' I said. 'It's moving through time. And space. It's subverting reality.' It's taking on our sins, I thought. The *mysterium iniquitatis*. It's eroticizing cruelty and death. 'Those Martians. Those heathens. They won't always be immune. They'll regret it one day, offering asylum to sex traitresses.' (The usual mutterings: 'A long-gone –' etcetera etcetera . . .) 'But you wouldn't understand. You're just humans. Hosts.' A pair of hands, small tentacular hands with long red claws, had settled on my pects. They squeezed, tweaking my nipples. And then, in affected kid-robot lisp: '*Yai* say you wan' see me.' Phin was at her best; she had stepped out of her flesh and into her lacquered, longing-to-be-Dresden look, all high-definition make-up and reformatory school ra-ra-ra. 'I am pris'ner of lust,' she said, her lustful artificially-plump lips rendered in magenta and glycerine to provide the illusion of lips wounded, much-licked, much-abused. The dress was a disease, a dying dermaplastic shimmy striped with mela-nomas, cinched at the waist with electrical flex; across the breast, GIRL #0978Z; when she moved, the sinistral, transgressive hemline promised a semi-otician of flirtatiousness a lifetime's work. 'Mr Loch-ester, he pris'ner too.' The sentient phallus slipped its leash; to George's outrage it climbed his trouser leg and boarded the bar, a little swashbuckler of true grit and gristle. 'But he *my* pris'ner. *My* slave.' Mr Rochester swaggered up to a beer glass; sub-merged his empurpled head; ejaculated. 'Sorry,' said Phin, swiping the detumescing Rochester off the bar. 'See people, get excited.' She re-secured him to the dog lead.

'Oh, this is too much,' said George as he and sev-eral of the bar's riffraff withdrew, nauseated, gag-ging. 'Bill, you've got voyeurs in your bathroom, rats in your kitchen and obnoxious, cantankerous dicks in your bar. C'mon boys, let's go over to Mama Robo's.' Turning to Phin, he added: 'Mamzelle, your slave needs discipline. *Strict* discipline.' Bill met my eyes, drilled them with hate as his best-paying customers left.

'Be nice to me,' I whispered. 'I have to impress this nana. I have to impregnate her.'

'Leave,' said Bill, his mouth about to detach itself from his face and fly homicidally about the room,

104

'lunatic. Just leave. Go root your sheila. Go, before you go completely *burlesque.'*

I took her to the Tsaloth Tsar, a floating restaurant on the Mekong river popular with status-hungry, transcom-toting young Thais for its ostentatious Khmer-Siberian cuisine. A waiter had her tether Mr Rochester outside. 'Feed to ducks,' he'd said, and Phin had treated him to a censorious *tui!* He was referring, of course, to a Thai woman's predilection for castrating an unfaithful husband while he slept, the method of disposal. *'Poot len, poot len,'* he'd added, laughing. Reassurance. He was being a wag. After all, her novelty penis was a collectible, an object of desire. The ducks would have to go hungry. But not us. I'd done a little surreptitious fingering of cash off Phin as we'd left the Zini.

'It's like this,' I said. The river, low and tranquil this dry season (though the dragon that slumbered in its depths would devour any swimmer audacious enough to tempt it), burbled past, black, speckled with plastic bottles and waste. 'I want you to have my baby.' Phin giggled; drowned her laugh, weighting it with dollars, Deutschmarks, cunning.

'If boy wan' marry, boy must have money. I think you write Mama, Mama send you every time, no?'

'Yes,' I said, lying as silkily as I was able. 'Did I

ever tell you my mother is a Martian?' Phin's eyes, gummy with mascara, unstuck, flipped open, became almost Caucasian, so wide they yawned at hearing this unbelievable news.

'Waiii! Iggy, you half Martian?'

'I'm a very rich man, Phin. An eccentric nanomillionaire.' Her cupidity, which was her most vulnerable fault line, the one on which I had chosen to exert pressure, trembled, ready to quake and raze her cynicism, her whore's contempt; the moment passed. Guardedly, she played her hand.

'But you doll junkie. Your jissom go bad.' Yeah. Mildewy. Rotten. But, I hoped, still good for making dolls. A spermatozoon, amongst that bayou of green slime, surely had my daughter's name on it.

'A weakness (*hélas*), a moment of weakness in a cricket pavilion near my old school . . .' First kiss, velveteen. When my humanity began to die.

'If we make baby, baby turn roboto when she first have *bpen-leut.*'

'True,' I said. 'True, and strange. The nanomachines in her genes' – I grinned a mad scientist's grin – 'would be activated by the pituitary gland, recombining DNA during menarche. By the time puberty is achieved a girl has metamorphosed into a doll.'

'Cool. But cyborg die young, no?'

'Well, yeah,' I said. 'Teenage holocaust. But listen: the British government will soon be paying lots of money to families who have dolls. In fact, a doll is going to be our new queen.' Phin's eyes flared, went supernova; jackpot, they said.

'Take me England?'

'I don't know. It's a crazy place.' But what did I know of England? London was my home, home of all those who had migrated down Europastrasse-55 through the flyblown ruins of the east; London, ghetto of Ossi refugees, prison to those infected with the doll plague; it was all I knew of my birth-land. But now, with this coup d'état and the cordon sanitaire being lifted . . .

'Have beauty shop in England?'

'I don't want you mechanized, Phin. I want you human.' She wrinkled her nose.

'You no wan' me like Lilim? Green eye, big teeth?' I shook my head.

'Lilim can't be manufactured. They have to be born of Man.' I looked across the river, to Laos; tiny coconut trees lined the distant bank like the stakes of a stockade I would never escape. Escape. It had often seemed to Primavera and me that we had spent our lives in a game of pursuit and escape, a deadly game in which the whole world was 'it'. In crossing the Mekong we had hoped to make escape final; we had hoped to rest. Ah. Too ironic. Too cruel. For Primavera, the Mekong had been the Styx. Play the inseminator, I told myself, play up and play the game before your junk-fried genitalia explode and you too are tagged. 'I've been addicted to Lilim for as long as I can remember. Imaginatively, at first. In nightmares and daydreams. Then physically. Then spiritually. It's going to be tough, fucking you. I want to thank you for all the effort you've made. The dress, the make-up, the gestures . . . I mean, you really look quite the *poupée*.' Phin frowned. 'I've had a tough life . . .' What did it take to melt her titanium heart? 'They treated us like dogs, rats, like monkeys. London was one big medical experiment. A laboratory that contained the plague.' Bites of sound, of vision, savaged my brain: the Rainham Marshes littered with the flotsam of looted suburbia, the moody depopulated streets, the howls, the screams amidst the ruins of the tower blocks, the razor-wire and the encircling, incarcerating walls . . . 'Drones hovered above us, recording the mutations, the deaths; the government justified itself by saying our freedom would mean the death of humanity.' I choked back a sob. Too amateurishly, I suppose.

'One fuck, five hundred baht,' said Phin, her face hard. 'You wan' marry, must give house, car, gold, money. Very much money.' Ho-ho, I thought, yes, and probably the bogey from my nose. 'And if have baby,' she continued, 'Queen of England, she must give money too.'

'Sounds fair to me.' She regarded me foxily, like a schoolgirl looking forward to dissection class; and then the metallic sloe-eyed stare became doe-like, yielding, as if she had reasoned there was no chance of cutting up the big, big bunny wabbit today.

'Maybe you speak good. We see.' She gave her concentration to the task of demolishing a plate of *som tam* and a tadpole suet. 'You look different, Iggy. Not so much like junkie. More like sex murderer.' I ran a hand through my crop. The bathroom mirror, that morning, had revealed streaks of grey; my face seemed longer, starved, with bony declivities and rills and angular, cubist masses. Despite the strange green discharge of last night, I hadn't felt so strong, so healthy, for years.

'Do you think it's possible,' I said, 'to premember things?'

'Pre-mem-ber?' She indulged me with a little frottage, one of those wild amberoid thighs frantic beneath the table. The town's PA was broadcasting something about rice prices, a coup perhaps ... 'Take me home, Iggy. Take me to your hotel and fuck me. But remember, darling, no play doctor, promise?' And all philosophical speculation was lost.

Afternoon:

The zzz of an unfastening zip: drowsy insect noise in a steel-plated jungle, roof cover of asbestos, no water, no earth, no sky. The hypo dropped from a rubbery vein, its needle glistening with blood and the reproductive materiel of Lilim. 'Hum job, Mr Telephone Man?' (No, no, that rap had run its course, I had to fill this nana with my sexual

109

nanoforce . . . Phin was only nine, but the 'ceuticals that had made her so mammiferously-o-matic had filled the trough of her hips with precocious womanhood; even without the evidence of the old rubber spoiler you could tell the little bitch was ovulating.) *'Diaphragm,'* I tried to say, hoping she hadn't switched to a contraceptive vaccine, *'take out the diaphragm.'* But my drug was in me and my tongue was lame. What dreams did you dream, Mr Rochester, curled up on the floor, of what rapes, what voluptuous terrors? Or were you as small-minded as your mistress, as venal as you were venereal, and nothing like Meta's own? The *Lao Kow* bottle thrummed like an electric pylon, a ventriloqual high-tension cable; in its magnetic field – a forcefield of sex and death – the future, unmuzzled, was talking to me . . . *'Dagon calling. Hello, hello? Come in. Come in, my shadow . . .'*

CHAPTER FOUR

Strange Grace

Shortly before she was due to die I summoned her to my rooms. There, after her handcuffs had been removed and I had dismissed the Imperial Guard (they exited to the fricative music of mesh on flesh), I ordered her to submit herself to my scrutiny. 'Stand,' I said. On hearing that command prisoners are required to place their hands behind their heads so that men (yes, my shadow, you may call me a 'man') may appraise their loveliness, or interrogate them. Of course, in the past, the dark morphosis of the past, the past appropriated by the future, before the female of our species 'civilized' us (so hypocritical this 'civility', this public relations exercise designed to ease the conscience of laissez-faire Mars), Lilim might be obliged to assume this position before being summarily executed, their proffered umbilici run through with swords. And it was, perhaps, an atavistic tic that made her glance, with bashful, flickering suspicion, at the ceremonial rapier that hung from my side. 'Stand.' I addressed her with the curtness one reserved for her kind.

She was prevaricating, tugging nervously at her hair, shifting her weight from one knee to the other.

'*No.*' Paradoxical word, so sweet on a victim's lips but like wormwood on the lips of a rebel. Fractious, sulky, she broke position; walked towards me, readjusting her torsolette (GIRL #0978Z emblazoned across the vertical monochromatic stripes); sat on my desk, leaned over, took off my glasses, breathed on them, then rubbed the lenses against the bruised cadaver-like plastic of her uniform before settling them on her own nose. 'My God, how do you *see* out of these?' I snatched the glasses back. 'Why Miss Frobisher,' she said, imitating my *ex cathedra* cadences, 'you're beautiful.' Her insolence – always her most devastating quality – rattled my composure, the sang froid of the Meta gentleman. No more games –

'Why did you do it, Vanity?'

'*Why did you do it, Vanity?*' The sarcasm wrinkled her nose, turned down the corners of her mouth. 'I'm psychotic. A pervert. Didn't you know?' And then, punctuating her explanation with a sigh, exasperated but resigned to the fact that I didn't know two plus two equalled five, added, 'Because you made me, of course.' She picked up the gilt-framed photograph of my first love. 'You can't forget her, can you?' True. True, and strange. She removed the petrified matrix from around her neck (we allow prisoners jewellery) and skimmed it across the desk,

112

a smooth oblong pebble, a piece of delicately-hewn malachite that clipped over blotting pad, papers, pens and ink (props, dandyish props; I always used the teleputer set in the wall) and came to rest in my lap. 'You can have it back,' she said. 'I'm through with it.'

'Primavera,' I said, depositing the matrix on the blotting pad, where it flushed, green and sickly, like a Rorschach Test suggesting the sex death of the universe, 'Primavera would never have betrayed me. Not all girls put to their knees go the Way of the Cat.'

'Primavera – tui!' She tossed her ponytail from one shoulder to the other. 'I did my best,' – anger out-reddening the rouge on her cheeks – 'I did my best to look like her. I had to. I went Meow! the first time we kissed. I was doomed.' And she fifteen now, too, to die the same age as Primavera. 'I did my best.' Re-engineered by Bangkok's surgeries, the pirated lines of the third-generation doll had given her – for someone who remembered such creatures and despite her body's rejection of the radioactive eye-stain – an erotic edge over her too-human contemporaries. But surgery had not refined the general into the particular. Her resemblance to my dead love – though she had gone so far as to have her speech centres rewired so that she spoke in cockneyfied Mitteleuropean – was only approximate.

'I liked you brown,' I said, lying desperately to

myself as much as to her (for Elohim desire not the feminine but the superfeminine). 'I like you white. I'm a sadist, not a racist.'

'You liked Loulou,' she said. 'You liked her green eyes.'

'I only saw her so that I might see you.'

'*Pak wan*.' Sweet mouth. Flatterer. '*Pak wan, kon prio*.' Sweet-mouthed, sour-bottomed. And my officiating over the firing squad would, I suppose, soon prove that proverb true . . . She eased herself off the desk, her rump leaving its damp signature on the glass top; walked about the room, a fingernail running over the spines of my library as she clove to the parabola of the walls, the filibustering click of her high-heels like a rusty clock, the tap of a blind man's cane.

'So you want to know why I did it?' Coy; a little girl who has just strangled the new baby and is about to boast; a schoolgirl who at last gets to dissect the big, big bunny. 'I did it *because* –' She leaned against the book shelves, a leg drawn up, one hand clasping the stiletto of a mule, the other caressing a tome of jurisprudence. 'Poisoning's so gauche; defecting to reality's old hat. I invaded the past because I have chosen, Dagon, in some universe other than this, to un-man you, to take away your inhumanity.' I lowered my eyes; the matrix winked at me, it seemed, as minx-like as my interlocutor. 'I invaded; I subverted. The past has been changed. Your past. One of them, that is. In that time-line

you take care of me. You're nice. We have kids . . .'
I picked up the magic uterus, felt the power, the
small, diminishing but mad, mad energies of the
vampire belly in my palm. 'As long as somewhere,
sometime, things are different . . .'

'We're not human,' I said. 'We can never be
human. You don't understand.' The room shook,
not physically, but as if withstanding the impact of
high-explosive cause-and-effect fired from outside
time, outside space; a multiplicity of futures, pasts
and presents irradiated the Spartan furniture, the
high curving bookshelves, the cupola decorated
with images of . . . who? Our first queen Titania
St Tallulah? Titania St Tabitha? Toxine, Trixie,
Trish? The image morphed, bewitching my
memory. And then the room itself dissolved
(though retaining its outlines, like leaded crystal),
the chambers and antechambers of countless
prisons swelling my vision with scenes of superimposed captivities, double, triple and quadruple
scenes of tortures, executions, criminal martyrs and
martyrs of crime suffering beneath the lash, hanged,
burnt, crushed, scalded, impaled by ingenious death
machines, each scene's rationale belonging to
unfathomed worlds and systems in the parallel uni-
verses of Meta. The blast of causation – contaminat-
ing time's arrow – mutated seconds into hours; an
attack by our double agents (the engines of uncre-
ation, the beautiful anarchs, one of whose sister-
hood I held in my hand), it represented another

incursion from unreality in its border war with the real. When the room again assumed its proportions its familiarity seemed fragile, as if Meta had deepened (though I knew it could not yet have consolidated) its hold upon the Earth. I placed the matrix back on the desk, an eldritch paperweight; drummed an aleatoric overture with my fingers.

'It's impossible for us to escape destiny, for me to be anything more than a killer, for you to be anything but a victim. Human history is being retrofitted. To accommodate Meta. To accommodate us. *All* time-lines, *all* human worlds. That we met six years ago in Nongkhai: don't you know that that event itself has become a dream? This moment will also soon become unreal. Soon, we and this moment will become less than ghosts, co-ordinates erased from the map of space-time. You've failed, Vanity, you've failed.' I crooked a digit; lazily, with puzzlement transforming her face from that of one who knows everything (and has grown tired of knowing) to that of a new-waif-on-the-block, she clicketty-clacked to my side. I rose, took her by the arm, my leather-gloved hand impressing bruises over the words *Staatlicher Porzellan Manufaktur Meissen*; turned her to the window. 'Six years – was Bangkok, this Bangkok, built in a mere six years? Did we become masters of the world in so short a time?' I pushed her forward so that her body pressed against the pane, one cheek flush against the glass, a startled eye – so black there was no demarcation between pupil and iris – regarding me from the residua of her epicanthic folds.

'I – I can't remember.'

'A CIA-sponsored coup. The Human Front deposed. Humans and Lilim forming a new presidium, a collective dictatorship with Titania its titular head. The kingdom reunited. A revolution, a civil war of organic against inorganic. The triumph of the dolls. And then an empire established, an Empire of Dolls, a Pax Britannica . . . All this in six years?'

'I – I can't –'

'History shifts beneath our feet. It's no longer we who travel through time and space; it's our ideas, our obsessions. We live relative to the velocity at which Meta infects the space-time continuum. And Meta's velocity is increasing even as we speak. We shall become timeless, non-spatial; observed but non-observing. We shall become fictions, the living dead of the new God.'

'Memories,' she said, 'where are my memories?'

Memories: my own had been corrupted. I had begun to forget who I was, who I had been. I looked out from the grey fortress of Lat Yao into the microcity, the little *urbs quadrata* of the interdiction, its neon crosshatches of roads and *soi* where humans scurried, surrendering themselves to or fleeing from the dart and flash, the thirst of my foraging sisters. From the drained lake beneath my feet, amongst its vegetable horrors and ferroconcrete wastes, rose tiny cries of pleasure, of pain. Sweet music, last bars of reality's finale, of history's rape . . . This is not the same interdiction that you suffered, my shadow; this *quartier* is under our control, controlled breeding being the raison d'être of the dead boy, reason and his prerogative. But something bigger than Elohim, bigger than any man, Homo sap or supe, is in control, ultimate control of our Fate, for holy Meta now infects not merely the human gamete; all time and space is metamorphosing into The Doll, a redemptive fiction wherein cruelty and death have been eroticized, converted, to turn, through millennia, aeons, through all eternity about love's green superluminous sun.

Memories: the narrative was disintegrating. Perhaps it was only my missionary zeal, the fact that I had been instrumental in initiating Metastasis, that allowed me to remember anything at all. I closed my eyes, crossed my arms about my condemned girl's breasts, codpiece snug in her perineal divide.

'We survive only through radical control of our population. Titania, our first queen, understood this. She made a deal with America . . .' Jack Morgenstern's shade whispered realpolitik into my ear:

'*What they proposed was this: Titania would send her runaways to countries of geopolitical significance to us. When the plague began to undermine those countries' economies, Titania would unleash what she called "the secret of the matrix". Only America would be privy to that secret, would recognize it, would know how to exploit it . . .'* I ran a hand from Vanity's plastic-wrapped breasts to the taut plateau of her belly (vibrant with its tom-toms of bellyblood); hidden, there, beneath the cropped vest of the torsolette, unprotected by its cloying second skin, was Europe's death-wish, a death-wish an original Cartier automaton like Titania had had the power to unlock but which now responded – pulse quickening, beads of sweat coalescing on her brow – to the touch, the scent of Elohim. 'The secret of the matrix,' I continued, 'was the secret on which they based their *konspiratsia.* America, out of national interest; the Lilim, to regulate population growth, to change their relationship with humanity from one of parasitism – which, unchecked, would lead to the extinction of both inhuman and human – to one of commensalism. It would give the recombinant a chance to live side by side with the species whose genitalia they needed in order to breed.'

The secret. I remembered floating down the Mekong, the ZiL out of control . . . Primavera had killed Morgenstern, but Titania had called out to her, called out over 10,000 kays, Die, die, die . . . Mental news reel images of US marines deployed to Venezuela, Iran, Korea, Australia, war ships delivering marble slabs, concentration camps filled with little witches who had surrendered to that same call . . .

'But then the first dead boys appeared.' (And the

secret that our species was in love with death was a secret no longer.) 'The Lilim changed. Together, we no longer needed America. Dead boys, dead girls – we had our own conspiracy . . .

'The matrices of the previous generation, though damaged by the spike, retained elements of quantum magic. We sold them, demonstrating how they could be modified for transdimensional travel. Sold them to America. To Europe. The Far East. Mars.' (I was, my shadow, an adroit and convincing salesman; how I regretted that [though I'd never disclosed our marketing strategy, so to speak] I'd practised my salesmanship on V, prising open a necrotic vagina, revealing the quantum wormhole [the 'Krafft-Ebing' black hole, as we say] running through a fourth physical dimension to the hyperwomb and its naked singularity. That wormhole, I would insist, could be made macroscopic. You just needed a good Martian engineer.) 'But the matrices lived their own lives,' I continued. 'The seed of our species – the self-replicating nanoware that had now miniaturized itself into something like pure information – had become self-organized, an independent entity, a form timeless, motionless, unreal; a spiritual entity, a demiurge, a god. Information determines space and time. And Meta – god of superluminal information – come to term, its gestatorial sojourn in the present complete, flowed through the transdimensional gates, flowed back through time, altering history to its own purposes.

America is ours, the world is ours as Mars will be ours, and all reality, when Meta attains its end.' The window, its drape of night sky, held our images like antique photographic plates of some anti-world, and we seemed like giant black angels bestriding a city of pestilence, a pestilence that was about to destroy its harbingers; faint, transparent, we were deliquescing into a forgotten, scarcely mythical point in time. The room seemed to tilt; giddy, I tightened my embrace about the girl-meat of breasts and abdomen, the only life that I knew would never be transubstantiated, the core of Meta itself.

'Why didn't you tell me? Why didn't you tell any of us?'

'And give you further scope for betrayal?' I sighed. 'We conspirators: we number only a few dozen. We don't tell others about our plot because Meta's triumph involves the destruction of our personae, each little history we call a soul, a soul that, as a wise man once said, is the prison of the body. We won't allow fear of the world outside that prison to create panic amongst the prisoners. We won't allow those who doubt our plans to sow ontological terror, terror of the new. Meta must, *will* be free, free of the metaphysical rack, the prison of human values.' I kissed the root of her ponytail, sneezed, the silk ribbon irritating my nose. 'Maybe we really did meet six years ago. Or maybe it was six hundred. Or six thousand. I'm not sure I know any more . . .' The room shook . . . Once upon a time there was a boy named Ignatz Zwakh . . . The past was infinite; our genesis, a never-to-be-reached future, this moment that was disintegrating even now . . . A moment that was becoming the past, a past that was the future. Ah. Amazing grace . . . Vanity had fallen to her knees and was using her teeth to unlace my codpiece. The grim reaper – so permanently, so painfully erect – sprang forth, punching her beneath an eye still puffy from her interrogation when she had first owned to invading time. (You beat them not to make them confess, but to correct their willingness, their over-eagerness to confess, you beat them to sift crimes true from untrue.) It had been a banal kind of interrogation; all interrogations were since we had been prohibited from using instruments of torture . . . Images of a gigantic pendulum swinging from one side of the prison to the other, a girl tied to its bob; the serrated beam a girl would be forced to sit astride; the wheel, the trussings, the choke . . . She betrays me; I hunt her down; she begs for mercy; I kill her. Perhaps that was the only constant in the flux of this multiverse. Primavera stared at me from her gilt-framed Polaroid, souvenir of a life when she was still half-human, before her metamorphic life on the run; her jealous butterfly soul fluttered above her wasted matrix. Once upon a time there was a boy named Ignatz Zwakh. There was a boy. Once upon a time. Once. Once . . .

My memory boils over with worlds, time-lines, murders; but out of the evaporating past these things still remain, though they seethe, close to vaporization:

A few weeks before they crucified her Titania had charged her envoy in Jakarta with the task of finding me (Thailand had yet to be colonized); it seems she had always known I was a dead boy, ever since those days when Primavera and I had sheltered in her underground palace amidst splendours pilfered from the abandoned *belle époque* shops of Bond Street and the King's Road, safe (we thought) in those endless corridors, stairwells and salons that were haunted by a thousand green luminous eyes. Along with Phin (who had, I think, already started to travel the *via Felis femella*), Mephisto took your narrator, still Ignatz Zwakh, back to London, to the *Seven Stars*. The palace had changed; it had begun to rise above ground, leaping into the dreary skies above Whitechapel and Aldgate. London had been opened (everything had changed) and was re-established as the nation's capital; only the East End was interdicted, but to keep humans out, not the recombinant in. When humans entered that forbidden city, it was by command, to feed my sisters and to fulfil the demands of our carefully regulated breeding programme . . . Think: my visit home, to the Rainham Marshes, to the tower block on the Mardyke Estate where I had grown up, a prisoner of the interdiction. 'I'm so proud of you,' Mum had said inside the vulgar compass of chez Zwakh. 'My baby, one of the rulers of the world.' Dad was dead;

he'd passed away in his dreamscaper while reliving the beautiful days of the *aube du millénaire*, their romance, their frivolity . . . The streets were not as empty as I'd remembered; people had started returning to the suburbs (the dispossessed, the disinherited and the carpetbaggers, of course), the wall, the surveillance of the killer satellites, the barbed wire and the machine-gun towers that had followed the ring road of the M25, gone, destroyed. I walked up the stairs of the tower block where Primavera had lived (the place had been ransacked during the last days of the Front), but Mrs Bobinski – a woman whose discomfiture at having a doll for a daughter had turned into detestation – was gone, and no one amongst the few remaining residents knew where. I went into Primavera's bedroom, took some clothes from her chest of drawers, held them to my face, inhaled deeply, and then, along with an old Polaroid of Primavera in her school uniform that had been pinned to the wall amongst posters of yesterday's pop stars, stuffed them into my pockets . . . And then I walked again to my old school, sat at the desk which had stood behind Primavera's, again imagined that half-metre of yellow-black hair, its scent, newly-washed, sweet. In the park outside I sat in the shadows of the cricket pavilion, touched my chest where her teeth had first entered my flesh. But I knew now that it had not been her kiss that had taken my humanity; I had been like her even then; for as long as I could remember I had dreamed

of killing girls; I had been born Elohim, dead . . .
Think: our college in the bowels of the *Seven Stars*,
the foundations of the new world, Titania's old
sanctuary. My feelings towards Titania had always
been cool; she was a ruthless politician; her strategy
to liberate dolls from oppression had, after all,
caused the deaths of millions of her sisters, one of
whom had been my love. But now that I was
Elohim, the blood-lust flowing more strongly
through me every day, I could, in part, appreciate
her devotion to Meta, her strange cruel principles,
her perverse integrity. In the end, she had given
her life for us . . . One day, in the middle of a tutorial
in the gym, while we were practising various
wounds on the college's inexhaustible supply of
shop-window mannequins (every Elohim, every
Lilim, remembers where he or she was that day),
we were interrupted by a stern-faced Mephisto who
announced that Titania had been arrested by the
presidium. That night the TV showed news footage
of her and her seventy-seven disciples crucified on
the walls of the *quartier interdit*, feet nailed to cross-
bars, wrists secured to the verticals so that each girl
looked like an arrowhead pointing the way to Hell;
and the *titulus* of each cross read 'Traitress'. They
used humans, doctors from the Dolls' Hospitals, to
perform the wretched task. For the last time I stared
upon the austere beauty of my queen. The camera
zoomed in, panned her ball-jointed limbs, the
immortal twelve-year-old face, the flawless body,

the green suns of the eyes. She had been built for the amusement of Europe's *nouveaux riches*, a toy, a marvellous toy, an automaton commissioned by the House of Cartier. 'Tricks,' said Toxicophilous, inventor of *L'Eve Future*, 'that is all they perform. Party pieces. Entertainments. *Feux d'artifice*!' But their inventor's dreams, his childhood nightmares of the chimera, the vampire and the sphinx, had found their way into his automaton's matrices, and *L'Eve Future* had begun metamorphosing into Europe's death-wish, the realization of Toxicophilous's darkest fantasies and desires . . . We college boys ran outside, even though we were supposed to be confined to our dorms, to see Longinus, our Lord Chamberlain, thrust his spear into Titania's exposed sex – a smooth rounded sex of porcelain that lacked a natal cleft – she unable to defend herself, her magic useless while the scent of Elohim filled her nostrils, her belly; blood filled the awaiting chalice as we sang *God Save the Queen*. It was a sad moment. It was a proud moment. In her death was our life. She had given us the future. Dying, Titania had at last become Lilith, mother not only of the succubi, but of the incubi . . . Think: wandering about the fur-lined halls and boudoirs of the ziggurat, salons crawling with girls – such narcissistic, spiteful, faithless little creatures – girls whom I was learning to hate as much as to adore. They spent their days lolling about in their rooms playing autoerotic games that seemed mostly to involve dressing up,

applying gallons of cosmetics and unmercifully teas-
ing the boys they knew were forbidden to hurt
them, the students whose frustration and pain they
savoured as much as (I suspect more than) the pain
of the human men, the 'polly-wogs' they raped each
night. Or else, surrendering to the miasma of boredom that permeated the nymphenberg, they would
confine themselves to the bedlam of their pleasure-
massacred beds, sleeping, eating, bingeing on goo-
goo, candy floss, fudge sundaes, chocolates and
syrup dips, killing the hours in mindless prattle
or by dreaming cruel masturbatory dreams . . .
'Incapable of love, all Elohim may expect from
Lilim,' said Mephisto, 'is respect. But oh, Elohim
may love Lilim . . .' My teacher would try to comfort me: 'Their promiscuity is necessary for the sur-
vival of our species . . .' And in the ziggurat at high
noon, its environs gridlocked with listless girls, I
would loiter in boudoirs, submitting to the taunts
of Lilim, and in my boyhood's appalling loneliness,
the appalling filthy loneliness of Elohim, would play
their stupid games, listen to their hysterical yaketty-
yak, smell the putrid scent of allure gone bad and,
hugging myself, know assuredly that one day there
would be revenge. It was that radiation of crimi-
nality that made me salivate, that I found such a
'turn-on', that made me want to kill; the vampires,
the girls who performed the exigencies of our
breeding-program with such dispatch, left me cold;
I desired only the rottenness of their sex . . .

Sometimes I caught that aroma when I would take a nocturnal stroll through the killing ground. In the ruins of the East End, the rubble-strewn, flyblown streets of the interdiction, beneath the great pile of the *Seven Stars* that towered over Whitechapel, Aldgate and Brick Lane, I would watch Lilim hunt down the men who had been offered to them that evening. Most aitch-men surrendered willingly; even those who tried to escape, would, after being bitten, tear open their incarnadined shirts and beg like sluttish street arabs (and yes, the girls always called them 'sluts') that their rape continue. Lilim prowled amongst the shadows, narcotic saliva dribbling onto their chins; though sometimes, sometimes, I would catch sight of a girl whose lips seemed stained with the unmistakable signs of dried semen. Such girls would hiss at me as I passed by . . . Think: Phin as a 'ward' resplendent in her new uniform. When a girl achieves metamorphosis (they made an exception for Phin who, despite her precocity, had still a few years to wait) she is entrusted to the care of an older girl until she reaches the age of sixteen. There is a similar system for boys (Titania had been collecting dead boys for over a decade), though we are called 'cadets'. Older boys, their metamorphoses complete, teach novices their skills, their mission; only on graduating does a cadet become a groom, a fully-metamorphosed Elohim. I was fortunate in having Mephisto to look after me. Mephisto the caged wild man, Mephisto the renegade . . . He was

like an older brother, the brother I had never had,
a role model, a father figure you might almost say.
Think: his tales (midnight-feast-in-the-dormitory
tales) of how he'd hunted nurses – not the kind
you encounter in today's nymphenbergs, but Lilim
who'd collaborated with the Hospital's paramedics
– and of how he'd brought them to the slab or else
killed and eaten them in the field; he would tell
of strange death machines, experimental machines,
the acid chamber, the spit, the clip, the scrag. And
I would fall asleep, my head on his shoulder. 'There,
there,' he would say, comforting me, 'they are very
sadistic, our little sisters. But the male-female
relationship in Meta is *necessarily* sadomasochistic
. . . We must learn to live with the rage in us, learn
to live with the dragon . . . Did I ever tell you about
Indonesia, Ignatz?' He often used my human name.
'It was in Indonesia that I learned who I *was*. It was
while watching a puppet show beneath the claws
of Merapi. My marauder sat by my side. It was a
shadow-puppet show, the kind the Javanese call
Wayang Kulit. All night we watched the puppets.
The sweetness of clove cigarettes mingled with the
mosquitoes. The puppeteer, the Javanese say, inter-
prets, like God, the shadows of war and faith. The
puppeteer offers meaning, he is the lantern's devo-
tee. "*But*," my marauder whispered, "*is he dragon-
master*?" We sat beneath the claws of that great
volcano and the serpent spoke: of how he would
bear down, a fiery worm, till we all were smelted

honey . . . The sun rose and my marauder and I knew that one day the dragon too would awake: the volcano, thick with blood, the ungovernable serpent. (Do not tempt his asceticism.) "Can song propitiate?" I asked the puppeteer, and he replied: "Demoniacal images guarded, once, the temples of passion. Those masks are lost. And the villages lie ignorant under stone. Accept. In time this murdering soil shall run through your fingers, so good. Its excellence, the mystery of Lord Shiva. His temples rise like stalks of rice. Rest, then, in a moment of abundance, watching the shadow-puppets, the gracious and the clown. The gamelan musicians take their cue. Cool rain pricks the skin. There is no fleeing his wrath, only a stillness in the half-light . . ." And it was then that man and marauder knew: we must always live at the feet of the dragon.'

'Tell us,' – it's Satan, the youngest boy in our dorm – 'tell us what humans are like without Meta . . .'

'Shadows,' Mephisto would say; then, understanding that the boy was calling on him to recite, the room would echo with his hieratic intonation:

Wrapped in blankets, they shuffle through cloud
greeting me in broken English. The people are
    scattered
and crawl towards their end, sparse as the
    mountain air.

Demise is roosting. It squats upon the plain
smothering the memory of hermit and priest
in the silence of these heights. Forgotten, that
   King of Mataram
who built those ancestral shrines. Then pilgrims
   came
to worship Shiva, climbing through scudding
   mist.
Pools of bubbling mud attended His presence.
The craters too, steaming, refulgent, cried out
   for
libation and prayer. The great stone phalli were
   drenched.
And once descending they found His fire
in wife, singing-bird and sword. Now the
   bubbling pools
give their death rattle. The craters are stale
and nightfall recalls men to their separateness.
Laughing, while children disentangle their kites
from the snares of telegraph wires, they think
of girls who have left for Surabaya
where the market stalls hawk penicillin.
They loiter about the temples, scratching words
upon the porch. The white man loiters,
cold and separate, then shuffles towards his bed.

'Goodnight,' Mephisto would say, 'goodnight,
sweet boys.' I liked Mephisto. I think we may even
have had sex. (Image of me lying prone on a cold
chequerboard floor, shirt pulled up, wriggling like

a dying sphinx ...) Everybody wanted to be
Mephisto's fag. (We would pick up on his sayings
– seeing a ward, a little schoolie passing by one boy
might say 'I can't decide whether to kill her then
eat her, or to eat her then kill her.' And we'd all
laugh. Ah. College days.) Memories swirl, draw me
into a blurred vortex ... Three years later, at the
debutantes' ball, I met her again. Think: swimming
pools filled with champagne. Fireworks. The two-
hundred-piece gamelan orchestra. (Mephisto had con-
nections.) The silverware. The porcelain. The games.
The tombola. (A caged aitch-man first prize, mag-
nums of blood second and third.) The pet leopards
and jaguars of those walking on the wild side.
The *cabaret d'mort*, the dominoes, the lorgnettes, the
masquers dressed as mermaids, gladiatorix, trapeze
artists, the bevy of punk-Marie Antoinettes. (And
we boys all in ecclesiastical black.) The girls who
asked us to feel their newly-trephinated sacra, 'In
case I'm naughty,' they said, and then slapped our
hands. Vanity shooed them all away ... 'I chose
Viridiana as my saint because I know you likee
2m!*&Zp!' (the biochip in her brain full of bugs
those days) 'girlykin *dtook-gah-dtah* with green eyes.
What *you* called now? Waiii! – you boys have such
silly names.' She lifted her stratocruising Directoire
gown, her belly undulating beneath the assault of
my two-fingered stabbing hand jive. La! (Fenrir
walks past; voices say 'Mmm. I wouldn't *mind* being
killed by *him.*' 'You mean only if you got the chance

132

to choke to death on his cock, you *cat*.' 'Dead is as dead does, sister.') When my hand jive upped the ante, three-fingered then four, she writhed on the dance floor in that house style popularly known as 'Die for the King.' ('I die, I die, I die!') Outside, on the parterre, I lifted her off her feet, eased my tongue into her umbilicus, deep, deeper; tasted there something going bad; and then, despite knowing that I was underage, that this was wrong (even then I had a marauder stirring in me), I nipped her breast, a breast firm, *al dente*, and lapped tentatively at the blood. She laughed with pleasure. I wanted to do more, of course; I wanted to stop her laughter; I wanted to go all the way; I wanted her allure. But I was a nineteen-year-old cadet, nervous, callow, frightened. (Had she been similarly frightened? Was she a fully-fledged cat, even then, who had been too apprehensive to ask to be put to her knees?) I contented myself with roughhouse kisses. Afterwards she told me she was on her way to Thailand to serve as translator and 'cultural adviser' to the new governess. I asked after Mr Rochester and was informed that he was dead (and knowing what I now know, he must have died in suspicious circumstances, poor Rochester likely being a victim of neglect, torture even, such is the vicious way these girls so often treat their pets). I gave her an ankle chain before she left. (She'd asked for my amulet, but that was something I was to concede only after I'd seen the effect Bangkok's surgeries had had on her, how

it had seemed Primavera had risen from the grave.)
Think: a year passes, two years, and then – not long
after the accommodation with Mars – I was expelled
from college for squelching this weird, suicidal nana
in a flea-bitten West London hotel . . . And this is
the hardest thing to remember . . . This is the hardest thing . . . The doting father dead, now, some
few months, perhaps her stepmother, a jealous
flint-hearted woman, a social climber stung by the
neighbours' constant gossip, had threatened to turn
that girl in to the authorities if she didn't submit to
a contract killing, in private, to protect the family
name (had hired me [though, of course, I'd refused
the money], she explaining 'all cats prefer to die in
a man's arms', well, of course they do, mother, of
course they do). Perhaps Cinders was just tired of
life, tired of being on the run, had come up to me
one night in the ruins of Bayswater, an *environ* still
as sparsely populated as during the interregnum of
the cordon sanitaire, and said 'Wanna kill a girl?'
Perhaps she wasn't so suicidal after all, perhaps I'd
tricked her (a scrambler on my belt), perhaps she'd
invited me upstairs for coffee . . . Introduction:
eight floors above Prince's Square she pours me a
demitasse, then tells me, in ritual fashion, her name,
height, weight, age, eye colour, measurements,
dress size. I feed her chocolate mice filled with green
semen. Or I take her out for one last night on the
town, drinks, restaurant, disco, late-night supper, a
taxi home where, after telling me, in ritual fashion,

her name, height, weight, age, eye colour, measurements, dress size, she slips into 'something more comfortable', emerges from her bedroom in fluffy mortuary black ... Or else I show her the gamekeeper, explain how dead boys could never contemplate using war weapons on Lilim; for girls, only the tiny high-velocity *fléchettes* that penetrate the body like the probosces of behemothic insects, the slim elegant bayonet, the exquisite harpoons; only these are good enough. And the knife? Yes, one of many. A beautiful combination of function and design – you like the dragon-figurative hilt? Thank you ... Courtship: we kiss. Fangs lock. She puts her arms about my neck. Or else, nervous, she backs away, then slowly (I am gentle with her) submits, slides into my embrace, rubbing herself against my leather doublet as if she were writhing in agony on the slab, and then begins to babble lewd nonsense ... She steps back, places her hands behind her head. The treaty with Mars has been signed and she thinks I am going to shoot her. Do I tell her of my intentions? I forget. It matters little. Engagement: I rive her. She is again in my arms. My left hand clasps her rump, my right ... I remember her eyes, her mouth. Always the same, wide-open, shock-stunned; a small noise at the back of her throat tries to escape; cannot. The blow has lifted her onto her toes. Mephisto would have been proud of me. And, after a pause, she says 'How could you?', or 'Why?', or 'Oh God, I'm ripped', or 'Bastard, you really shouldn't have *done* that'. Nuptials: I torture her, using knife, sword, bayonet etc., bending her over a stool, a window sill, dragging her across the floor by her hair ... The middle finger of her right hand covers her mutilated sex in coy masturbatory pose. She tells me she admires my gynaecological expertise. Thank you ... Briefly, I become her, she becomes me. (A cipher, pure superego, I thirst for selfhood, assume her suffering, her ego; while she, sitting in judgement on herself, becomes a cipher, a superego, confirming her own perversity.) Honeymoon: she's on the table now, ankles pinned behind her ears, or else I'm standing up, holding her broken sex to my mouth, consuming the allure of her corruption, resisting the impulse to tear and rend with my fangs, remembering Mephisto's dictum that unless we control the marauder, the wild man in us, we will destroy ourselves by exterminating the female, the seed-carrier of our people ... Half-dead, she feeds on me, on her knees, on her belly, inverted in my arms ... For both of us feeding is a semiotic rather than physiological act ... Metasex is metaphysical ... Divorce: it's the *off* that betrays her. I mean, a lady'd say 'finish me' not 'finish me *off*'. That's cat-talk. That's trashy. But I'm tired and I administer the coup de grâce anyway, shooting her through her heart ...

I was found out. The charge was serious: only alumni are allowed to kill, and this was a kill that violated an interplanetary treaty. I was told that I would have to spend several years in a hardship post. Older boys, like Mephisto, who hated Martian interference, and even some of the girls, I think, were sympathetic. I was allowed to choose my posting, and, of course, I chose Bangkok, City of Angels, for I often thought of my little magdalene, my fallen angel, the girl-child Phin, or Vanity. Abroad, I became part of the cabal working to recruit time and space to our cause. (It was my way of trying to redeem myself.) Abroad, Vanity turned – via a kind of second metamorphosis perpetrated by Bangkok's glamour physicians – into a simulacrum of an Occidental doll; and I turned Vanity into the notorious fallatrix who knelt before me now. The beauty of her first dollhood had not been good enough for her; she had wanted the beauty that ends in death. In her I recognized the archetype of the victim, the Plastic Venus, Logos of the Age made flesh, whose first incarnation had been my childhood sweetheart, Primavera; and, playing her emergent role with enthusiasm (I would invite her to my rooms in Lat Yao, to parties, dinners, trips to the beach), committing small, then larger indiscretions, crimes civil then capital, she would find herself at my feet, begging for forgiveness, a victim *manqué*, as if her body's conversion was only a prequel to this metaphysical conversion, this psychotic rehearsal for the sex death she coveted with all her doll-twisted heart. I could not resist that archetype, the dark anima that had haunted my childhood, claimed me in pubescence and now sought my destruction in manhood. As she became addicted to her own poisonous ways so I became addicted to punishing her delinquency. How could our affair have ended except in a consummation of guilt and prosecution, love and hate?

You know the rest . . .

'Daddy,' murmured my poor, condemned girl, 'Daddy, Daddy.' She knelt before me as she had knelt three weeks ago as Bardolph had passed sentence, one of many who had been condemned that day:

Adelle St Alceste
Amoret St Andromeda
Andrée St Annette
Angelique St Annabella
Ann-Marie St Anastasia
Belinda St Beatrice
Bunny St Bianca
Bunty St Bella
Candy St Cassandra
Cardine St Charmian
Carmen St Columbine
Catherine St Candice
Cherry St Celeste
Christine St Christabel
Claudine St Camille
Cleopatra St Clara
Daisy St Diotima
Debbie St Duessa
Delphine St Delphina

Dolores St Duessa
Dusty St Diane
Effie St Euphemia
Elanor St Electra
Fanny St Frances
   (the notorious 'Fanny the Fran')
Faustine St Fabienne
Fifi St Fabiola
Gigi St Georgina
Gillian St Gina
Griselda St Gudrun
Heather St Hella
Hermione St Helen
Honey St Hyacinth
Iman St Iphigenia
Ivy St Io
Jaqueline St Jaquenetta
Jezebel St Josephine
Judy St Jocasta
Juliet St Judith
Kate St Kristina
Kiki St Klytemnestra
Lindy St Lynsey
Lisa St Lysette
Lizzie St Lydia
Lucasta St Laura
Lysette St Lucrezia
Madeleine St Minette
Maria St Marie
Melanie St Mirabel
Melissa St Maria
Minette St Madeleine

Modesty St Maeve
Mona St Miranda
Nancy St Ninette
Nathalie St Nastassia
Nina St Natasha
Odette St Ornella
Patience St Pavlova
Penelope St Porphyria
Rachel St Rosita
Raquel St Rosaline
Samantha St Seraphina
Scarlet St Sacharissa
Sophie St Sophia
Tabitha St Titania
Tiffany St Tatiana
Tina St Trixe
Toxine St Tara
Trisha St Theresa
Trixie St Tina
Vanity St Viridiana
Venus St Viola
Vivienne St Vanadis
Wendy St Wanda
Yvonne St Yvette
Zenobia St Zika

Ah. Girls, girls, our enemies and our loves. (So
many girls, Mephisto would say, and so few of us.
Millions, millions; and us? Less than a thousand.
But Meta is wise. How could it be any other way?
For the male and female of Meta to survive, the
discrepancy must be thus.) They were Thais, mostly

(*farang* held only the senior positions in a crown colony), and would normally have been addressed by their *cheu len*, or nicknames; but the ceremony of death required formal rules, formal rhetoric. Their crimes? One girl – oh, I forget which – had taken to planting bombs beneath Bardolph's car (me, Bardolph and our sergeant at arms, Anubis, we look after the whole of Siam, though there's this little Thai kid, Ravanna, first Elohim to be born out here, that we've taken to baby-sitting); five times she'd blown him up and each time he'd lost arms, legs, his stomach once; limbs and organs it'd taken months to regrow. I remembered how, at her arraignment, she'd made the familiar defence that Titania herself had been a fellatrix (all those Big Sisters were); but Bardolph had replied with a curt 'Titania's dead.' Besides, I'd felt like adding, Titania had only become a true cat, a traitress, when her work on this planet had been done. She gave her life that we might have life: she sanctified the manner in which male and female interrelate: Lilim must die to feed Elohim; Elohim must feed so that Lilim may live . . . Another girl – this was Cherry, yeah, the coprophagous Cherry-ola, I'm sure – used an exceptionally unpleasant nanoware poison on two visiting Elohim (here for trade talks) that recombined their body chemistries into a) a grand piano, and b) a toilet. (We still haven't located the toilet. Poor bastard. Somebody is probably shitting on him right now . . .) Not that we have to deal

with many murderesses. Not murderesses of
Elohim, anyway. Despite all this chic talk of poisoning, most girls prefer to inflict psychological rather
than physical harm. (Only the really far-gone feline,
they say, can bear to draw blood from the dragon.
And by that stage a girl is usually derelict, a drooling
slavering *thing*.) There'd been, of course, that girl —
what was her name — who had preyed on her *own*
sex. (She'd this little Indian tailor in Pratunam
who'd run her up clothes from the de luxe flesh
of her victims.) Now I know dermaplastic's out of
fashion, that this season's look is all Real Thing,
but —

'Daddy,' mewled my fetish-object, my recurrent
twenty-five-hour-a-daydream, my dirty habit, my
girl, my love. I wound my fingers about her ponytail
(a half-metre of bleached hangman's rope), jerked
her head backwards. Her eyes closed, *clink!* like a
doll's, a tin doll's; her lips parted, saliva running
down her chin. This would be our last time together,
our last fatal intimacy. Bardolph had been generous — he would allow me to officiate over the
execution — but I would then have to report to the
governess. And I knew that bob-haired twenty-one-
year-old matron planned to put me on ice . . .
'Daddy. Please, Daddy. Mercy. I beg you —' I was a
student again, and Mephisto was telling me about
the birds and the bees. We were looking through
a two-way mirror at Elohim and Lilim locked in
metasex: 'The physical pleasure is, of course,

incidental, a brief reprieve from our constant pain, which, as we grow older, intensifies and will, I deem, be the thing that finally kills us, driving us mad, so that we die like our ephemeral sisters, no matter how many centuries it may take. Observe: by transforming a vampire into a cat men change the brother-sister relationship enjoyed by Elohim and Lilim into a father-daughter relationship, that is, a power relationship; it is in playing this power game that Lilim may reveal themselves to be criminals, girls who would undermine our discipline, turn against us, rebel simply for the frisson of rebellion, who would allow their appetites to take them beyond the interdiction, into the world, and so decimate the human gene pool. And without humans, Dagon, there would be no Meta. The cull is necessary for the continued existence of humans and inhumans alike . . .'

'But Daddy,' she says, as if reading my thoughts, 'I wasn't spreading the plague. Mars is immune. I became a traitress because I wanted to die. You made me a traitress because you wanted to kill me. Let's not make any more excuses, offer any more rationales. We're both mad, you and I: you want to kill as many girls as you can and I want to be one of your victims. Meta is self-consuming. We eat you, you eat us. Eat, eat, eat, eat. That's all there is, Daddy. That's all there is to Meta. I don't want to hear any more lies . . .' And then her cat-talk ceased as I filled her mouth . . .

Phin had assumed full lordosis, head buried in my crotch, back arched, rump in the air, thighs splayed. As she hummed me (hmmm! hmmm! hmmm!) the room palpitated, shook, the walls becoming transparent so that I saw into a transcendental number of prisons. And in one, a girl walked across a courtyard. Unbuttoned her blouse. Unhooked her brassière . . . Pose 1) She stands, one knee bent, hands behind her head, fingers entwined, her blouse, open to the waist, a corona of organza and lawn surrounding the pale, almost phosphorescent breasts that are petitioning, begging for oblivion. Pose 2) She stands, knees flexed, hands clenched behind her ponytail, fingers tangled in hair, wincing, the mouth extravagantly ovoid, a dribble of blood oozing from the small hole in her cleavage, a painterly brush stroke of scarlet brilliant as the creamy moonlight refracted by her sweat. Pose 3) She kneels, head flung back, breasts thrust towards the rigid, stone-faced firing squad, the five US marines (humans chosen to execute, though not officiate over her death, to add to her humiliation), mercenaries who have been able to overcome their dread of killing Lilim only by not knowing which rifle carries the single live round; breasts thrust supplicatingly, perhaps, but at the same time thrust to taunt, her superfemininity, her dollhood, having the power, even in death, of hurting them, of reminding them of what they cannot be, what they cannot possess. Pose 4) She lies on the ground, half

144

on one side, legs tucked beneath her, arms above her head, a brassière cup that had a moment before hung useless aside the left breast now covering, as if provoked by death's immodesty, the lewd wound, the scarlet letter of the traitress . . . Hup. Tongue flick in anus, scrotal lick, bite root, take the loot, eat me pussycat, eat-gargle-and-cry! Phin screamed (a nice, easy listening scream), screamed as if she caterwauled, screamed a long cat-crazy Meow!, broke from my grip and spat onto the floor. When she faced me a spume of green slime hung from her lips. '*Wha* –' It hurts, I know, I thought. It stings. It burns. But you'll get to like it. Like it so much that you'll move to Treachery Street. You're young. A babe in arms. (Though the hormone supplements you take have provoked a kind of half-metamorphosis.) Yeah, you'll get to like the icky green stuff, in time. In a choreographed display of disgust (this is how you ridicule a man, says Granny, this is the Terpsichorean art of sexual mockery) she was collecting her bag, her clothes, her sentient phallic friend – Calm down, I was saying, I've got something to tell you, something passing strange – she all the while reciting programme notes about how much she despised doll junk inadequates, their dirty compromised genes. 'I think you very bad for Thailand,' she said. 'You *monstre sadique*.' Her road to fully functional fourth-generation dollhood was going to be a road to Damascus.

'Don't persecute Meta's servants,' I said. She

performed a *jeté* through the door, her decomposing chemise held across her body like a mould-eaten bath towel.

So much for time-loops.

Time was no longer sequential; past and present had stalled; everything had been requisitioned by The Future.

'Hey, little girl,' I called, 'you got the *future*.'

And so had I.

I proceeded to get drunk.

CHAPTER FIVE

Strange Times

Jesus. Some bender. My trousers were on back-to-front. I stank of *Lao Kow*. And the room was poltergeist country. A half-cremated cat, servomechanism protruding from its skull, was suspended from the ceiling by one of the old school ties with which I sometimes handcuffed the occasional whore. Now, what was that all about? Tentatively, I raised my head. Jesus, thank you, thank you, no hangover, no pain. I rolled over; Primavera, I thought, we have to talk. I picked up the wombtomb; stroked it, cracked voice rendering what I could remember of that zygodiddly song (a song that celebrated psychotic zygotes) by last year's band, the *Imps of the Perverse*: Git bitten, git drugged till ya humanity fail ya,/Ain't no way out when ya got strange genitalia . . .

Memories. The past was dissolving into my memories of the future. If Meta was the allure, allure that had changed reality, then The Future was a state of mind. Before long, we would all be seeing things differently. The matrix radiated its green-light Go. Yes. I knew what I was. Not washed-up, not crash-landed; I was Meta, a dead boy. I had always been Meta. I pushed Primavera's bargain-basement mausoleum aside. 'I'm sorry,' I said. 'I'm sorry I didn't fulfil my promise. I'm sorry I didn't pass on your software. But things have changed. I've changed. And there's nothing I can do about it . . .'

I got up. It was time to go home. I had to go to college. Study female anatomy. Had to study ballistics, statistics. It was time to start living again. But first I had to get my head together. My memory repaired. It wasn't enough to know *what* I was; I had to learn *who* I was, too. I smashed the *Lao Kow* bottle at my feet, rescued the CPU, shook it dry and brushed the splinters from its tissue, its plastics and steel; tied the cyber-organic meat about my throat with the necktie that had exhibited the burnt-out moggy; swept out, stage left, to Shakespearean alarums. Leaving the *Mut Mee*, plunging into the sweltering night, all seemed lost behind a shrill opera of cicada song, the *took-eh* of house lizards, street vendor's cries and a mind brimming with thanatalogical dialectic . . .

Wat Khek was more than a temple. It was a sculpture garden. And a datamart, a cheap emporium of dreams, themes and the collective mind. I thirsted for its memorabilia . . .

The town was quiet, here, near the city limits; the day's carnage – a smashed bus, a torched motorbike, dogs with rigor mortis, little paws sticking in the air, hit, run and abandoned children – filled the irrigation ditches that ran parallel to the road. A rusted hovercar waited in vain for Mars to lift its embargo on liquid metallic hydrogen. (Some bottles of synthetic gasoline had been discarded on the hard shoulder; but you couldn't run a hovercar on that; all that engine-rot was good for was blanketing the waterways of Bangkok in a black, deadly smog; the West had banned it.) I passed the bug factory: 10,000 tonnes a day of ants, flour-beetles and grass-hoppers: an entomorphagist's utopia. The night breeze carried a bass note of wood and manure . . . A queue of pregnant women parted, allowed the trishaw to pass. They were filing into a fast-life out-let, a franchise that sold the ovaries of aborted foetuses to Bangkok's underground nanoindustry. (Unlike the automata of the *belle époque*, gynoids are not grown from the stuff of strange science but from womb-robbed, mechanized genes . . .) The trishaw left the river's conurbation, its bunkered population shell-shocked from a hundred years of slash-and-burn bizniz, turned off the Phon Phisai road and bumped along a dirt track until floodlit, spiralling concrete representations of snakes, Buddhas and Hindu deities rose from behind a veil of coconuts and palms. I entered the compound through the graffiti scarred mouth of a gigantic

149

cobra. Snakes. The abbot had a passion for snakes. He was, after all, the snake king, a man who had enjoyed a million years of majesty; his followers claimed that he could shape-shift. If only, they had told me, if only I had faith, I too could witness this miracle. But I hadn't come to Wat Khek to see an old man slither about in the sand; I'd come to access the Fujitsu in the library. I paid the driver and walked through the maze of ferroconcrete sculptures towards the *hong samut*.

Phra Bamrung appeared from behind the representation of an elephant and a procession of monkeys, monkeys with guns, monkeys gambling, drinking, whoring, monkeys in little Mercedes Benzes and monkeys dancing the *ramwong*. 'Mr Ignatz,' said the monk, 'snake-king want to know why you not come to rehabilitation centre?' Bamrung had once doorstopped me in the Café Mental for not availing myself of his detoxification treatment. He gestured towards the island, awash in a sodium glow, and its hospital that stood like a little Alcatraz in the middle of the Wat's artificial lake. Cages of morphine and heroin addicts, alcoholics and pillheads, called out to me for help. Monks struck the cages with steel bars; pulled one patient into the open (as if he were meat in some human abattoir), belaboured him with punches, kicks, PVC pipes filled with ball bearings. The unfortunate addict soon resembled a sitter for Francis Bacon's ghost.

150

'I don't like hospitals,' I said. Bamrung's lips tight-ened in a humourless smile. Careful not to make any ambiguous movements (I could see the bulge of a lightstick beneath the redundant sanctity of his robes), I again began my walk towards the library. 'I just came for information.'

'But you are doll junkie, Mr Ignatz, no?'

'I'm turning into something else.' Unable to resist a parting sally I added: 'Pretty soon, you'll be turn-ing into something else. Meta is going to colonize the Earth.'

'Thailand has never been colonized!' he shot back. 'We don't want you here! Before *farang* come, Thailand very nice place! Not have prostitution, not have drug! And *farang* lady – she very bad! Always want fucky, fucky, fucky! Fucky with everyone, even *samlor* driver! You have no god! All you think about is money! Dink, dink, dink, dink, and all time say dirty thing about Thailand! Go home, *farang*, go home!'

The lobby walls were covered with photographs of the snake-king's ancestors, the men all exhibiting dead reptilian eyes (I thought of Mr Rochester), the women the pinched aspects of those who suffer from congenital vaginismus. Behind the photo-graphs, I knew, in sealed recesses, were heads in cryonic suspension, refrigerated blood awaiting repeal (or for interest to compound into a waiver) of an overpopulated Thailand's anti-reanimation and anti-cloning laws. I tossed some fric onto the reception desk (a few baht for this poor man's AI with its limited access to the Net) and took the stairs to the first storey. Directional arrows guided the prospective user along a hallway stacked with artefacts illustrating the Wat's illustrious past: animist charms and fetishes; human skulls that had been dipped in gold; swords; daggers; the booty of organ traffickers from the years when the Wat had provided a haven for mentally retarded kids; bottled miscegenetic impedimenta to citizenship; the Harvard Business School Diploma of a famous transsapient trans-sexual; microcephalic crania, Negroid and Slavic, from the Wat's School of Oriental Eugenics; M16s; thump guns; artfully stuffed snakes; the bullet holed hyperskirts of Vietcong a-go-go girls; pamphlets on AIDS; more pamphlets on AIDS; a visitor's book filled with the signatures of generals, minor aristocracy, plutocrats and pornocrats; more snakes; a mothballed saffron robed telerobotic droid once operated by the Tourism Authority of Thailand . . . A woman in a snakeskin bodystocking held an arras to one side; the cubicle was dark; I settled myself amongst the cushions.

As I tied on the bandana, tightening the velcro so that the electrodes were snug against my brow, the big monitor that hung from an invisible wall awoke, snowstormed. The Fujitsu had no walk-in mode but was still relatively simple to use. It translated the electrical currents my brain generated as

I mentally prepared to vocalize, anticipating instructions by reading the symbolic representations of the concepts behind my words, concepts that were universal, regardless of language. *Dagon*, I thought, *Elohim with cross references*. The Fujitsu scanned the codes etched by an STM on one of the Net's vanadium-bronze pinhead disks. The monitor displayed an image of the fish god of the Philistines. Then the image blurred and for a moment I was seeing double, my own face, older and not-quite-human, superimposed on the original image. Pixels resolved and my big brother attained hegemony, filling the screen with a melancholy half-profile. '*Lord Dagon*,' said a voice inside my head, '*born 1956, Gabriel Strange, in north-east London, Great Britain, to Stanislaus and —*' Stop. Yes, yes, the past was being tampered with. I was being tampered with. Primavera — I fondled her remains — we really need to talk. But really. '*Primavera Strange.*' The screen projected the face of the sweet cheat, Miss Primavera Bobinski. '*Twin of Gabriel, died —*' Stop. Control your thoughts. Think: Dagon. Lord Dagon. Think: Elohim. '*Born 1956, Gabriel Strange, in north-east London, Great Britain, to Stanislaus and Raissa. Cadet 1972–77. Sent down for sexual perversion —*' Stop. So: I'm born 1956 instead of 2056. And my name's changed. And Primavera has become a sibling. Think: Bangkok. A ziggurat. A Bugatti. A girl. Tell me the story. Give me the facts . . . *The skyway was a convolvulus of shadows, a helix entwining a ziggurat*

153

of smoked glass from penthouse to the killing ground of the streets . . .

The Bugatti (a 1931 Bugatti Royal *Berline de Voyage*) skidded, fourteen-foot wheelbase banked into the vicious incline of the screw. Rain sprayed through the open window; the smell of burnt rubber was like the smell of burnt skin. The second explosion compressed his eardrums into the middle of his head; compressed, then transposed, so that, for an instant, he heard in inverted stereo (though imagination, not light, stained his retina with a clip of the governess, her eyes painted like Elizabeth Taylor's in *Cleopatra*, her hair like Betty Boop's, dead, blown apart, her boudoir in flames, maids and secretaries wounded, convulsing); debris beat upon the Bugatti's roof. 'Nobody's going to ice *me* for fifteen years,' he screamed, his voice a hybrid of the contemporaneous John Lydon's and a young apocryphal Peter Lorre's. The nymphenberg's lights dimmed, switched to auxiliary. Fourth level, third level, second . . . He wrenched at the handbrake as if at a mane of teased yellow hair; the car spun one hundred and eighty degrees, grazed a crash barrier, lurched then corrected its roll; the night whispered a vertiginous threat. Roadblock? He gunned the engine, glancing to where the gamekeeper lay refracting the kaleidoscope of the dash. *Crack.* A wing mirror shattered, shards replicating the image of an imperial trooper into infinity. (Fashion note: Faustine wears black PVC thigh boots, matching evening gloves with tines and retrogenic [some palaeontologists would argue mythopoeic] shark-tooth zippered *cache-sexe*. All by Allen Jones thru Junior Gaultier. Spiked collar and bodychain by Barbie Barbarossa. Biker's cap by Harley Davidson. Steel tipped bullwhip by Madame X.) He accelerated skywards, back window disintegrating in a comet-tail of glass as the Bugatti clove to the wall of death. The roller skating posse that rounded the cumber with fatal synchronousness was scattered, one girl dragged by the Bugatti's running board until the car – out of control now, lurching right then left – threshed her beneath the barbed shaft of its back axle. The Bugatti demolished the inner barrier, pitched into space, stalled, the axle, with its ribbons of PVC and pulped flesh, snared in the wreckage. A reflex (his loins informing his brain) made him grab the gamekeeper as the bonnet dipped; his prospect of a black vista of glass modulated to a well of black nothingness. He cartwheeled through the wind-screen, through the hot wet void, cyber-organic body punching a hole through the ziggurat, his ungainly trajectory redeemed by a perfect landing as if he were a gymnast completing a vulgar yet inhumanly spectacular display. God, he thought, taking in the skin-rag opulence of the décor (school of Georgette Heyer/Bob Guccione), the slit eyed figures in its landscape, God, Mmm, Yeah: Pyjama

Party. He fired from the hip, the gamekeeper flicking its long orange-white tongue towards the assembled girls, a lewd invitation to a different party, one that would last all night. (Fashion note: Dtim wears a black nylon baby-doll night-gown by Little Demoness; Uthai the same, in shocking pink; mules with padlock motif by Strangeways. Noi wears diaphanous harem pants with matching bolero by Fatima Fatwa; omphalos stone by Belly Belly Nice; gold safety pin by Oh So Vicious. Gung, It and Som wear black chiffon full-length shrouds with rose and poppy appliqué at the breast; pubic decals of fungi, belladonna and convolvulus; courtesan wigs [after Fuseli], respectively 100,000 volts, 500,000 volts and National Grid. All by Vampire Brats.) A *fléchette*-pocked maintenance spider exploded, the fusillade chewing up the mock-Regency furniture, breaking crockery, mirrors, porcelain Columbines and Pierrots, ripping the canvas of a Fragonard ('Girl Kneeling on Miniver'), spattering blood across the fur-lined walls, a film of allure hanging in the air like a frozen scream of pure Form, the Idea of all screams, all cries for mercy and forgiveness. Cordite and the faint smell of rotting fish and mouldy cheese (some girl here a traitress) mingled with the scent of atomized cells and plasma, all that was left now of six brief lives. Rewind. Play. (Captions by Interzini Incorporated.) *Girl jut abdomen, greet kiss of bullet, imitate sex death of Nastassia Kinski in Polanski's* Legend of St Viridiana. (Remake of Buñuel's 1930 silent classic starring Jean Harlow.) *Girl wiggle bust like Vegas showgirl as game-keeper treat her to impromptu double mastectomy, press body against David Bowie poster (Elohim-lookalike phase), chew David's pink three-inch stacks. Girl with safety pin in her ear unzip harem pant walk onto bayonet pretend he Sid, she Nancy.* (Be yourself, brown sugar, he thought, pulling the blade free, I don't care for *cultural* colonialism.) *Girl rend wet sticky chiffon as gunfire bisect torso from pubis to throat, strike pose of antique Thai dancer.* That's more like it, baboids. Give me grace, give me elegance. *Girl die a-go-go.* Yeah, get ethnic. Go, baby, go, go, go-go-go . . . He noticed the cake with its sixteen candles and thought, Mmm: always wanted to be a birthday killer. *Girl, alive but mortally wounded, drag herself through thick pile of carpet towards bed. Like bug, leave glistening slime-trail in wake. He shoot her before she reach sanctuary.* Despite the affair in Bayswater, the incident on Mars, he was little more than an initiate as a marauder. Traditions still bound him; he would not have been able to kill a girl on her bed . . . His ear caught the rumble of roller skates above the *luk tung*; he made to shoot the music centre; instead, seeing the *farang* tapes scattered about the floor, ejected the cassette featuring the wailing Isan cowboy and replaced it with the latest from *The Stranglers*:

Jack said Jill let's walk this hill
let's go get a pail of water,

and I won't frown if I crack my crown
so long as you come tumbling after. Ha!

Chorus: Meta, Meta, Meta, Meta,
   Meta-morphosis,
can-ya, can-ya, can-ya, can-ya tell me this:
Why should a man feel like Desperate Dan
when Meta go give him *nur-ser-y psychosis*.

Mickey dressed Minnie in a pin-pin-pinny,
Min was Mickey's little scullery maid,
and Minnie felt the zap of a rodent trap
every damn time that Mickey got laid. Ha!

Chorus: Meta, Meta, Meta, Meta, etcetera
   etcetera . . .

He pogoed over a body; jinked across the floor;
fired through the broken window. (Wished now he
had that bomb, his last, that he'd left in the Bugatti.)
A girl fell shadow-wards, her caterwaul shifting into
a brief shrill coda as she was impaled on the *cheval-
de-frise* of the palace ramparts. Recruiting cats, he
thought; fools. A cat'll bite the hand that feeds her,
no matter how strong the scent; for a cat all men
are to be betrayed; but if men turn girls into cats,
cats turn men into marauders . . .

Dr Who said, 'Fu Manchu,
Your brides need exter-min-ating.
The cruel hijinx of those five little chinks
deserve a Dalek's armour plating. Ha!'

The magazine was empty. He switched to harpoons. Of the five little chinks on the skyway he bellied one, breasted two, took one in the small of the back (that was a new thing, shooting a girl in the back; he liked it), took another through the rib-cage. (Fashion note: The dead all wear hypertenuous pinafore dresses in shocking pink and matching pink blazers, white blouses, and berets from Vivienne Westwood's 'Schoolgirl Slutz' collection. Stockings by Polly Wolly Doodle. Shoes by Dolls 'R' Us.) What do you think of this then, Vanity? I'm a sex criminal now, too . . . The vandalized Fragonard upbraided him, that girl sitting on her heels on the miniver rug, a girl corseted, stockinged, beribboned in whites and pinks, eyes fixed on the black velvet cushion on which the executioner's apprentice was placing the broad, serrated blade (the cushion he is about to offer to his master), that girl seemed about to say, What is the life of a marauder compared to this? How can you renounce such sacerdotal justice? His fangs extended. But no time to eat; run, run, he thought, Bardolph and Anubis will be here shortly. He moved into the corridor. The doors on either side of him were bolted; several nurses – probably answering the emergency call of a mad twenty-one-year-old; one carried a straitjacket – caught by surprise and denied safer haven by the corridor's occupants, were clawing at the teak-and-leather doors crying 'Marauder! marauder!' He loaded a fresh magazine; crisply starched uniforms turned into used blotting paper as the girls tangoed, waltzed, twisted and pouted to the gamekeeper's ludicrous fifty beats to the bar. (Fashion note: Sanitsuda, Mai, Nid, Joy and Boo wear international black-cross attire from Sin Sick Sisters of Bedlam.) Out of ammunition, he threw the gun aside; drew his pistol, his sword. He lost the sword almost straightaway: a door opened to his left – a voice shouted, 'Wantanee, no, close it, *close* it!' – and he was confronted by a ward with her Vivienne Westwood dress pulled up and over her head, the generous offer of a deep, dark umbilicus. As he watched her turn back into the room, hands on the hilt pushed flush against the entry wound, the rapier's long blade emerging from the elastic curvature of her back, he sighted the other girl, the ward's mistress, a Coca-Cola-headed Eurasian who screamed '*Yut Tanhasadist!*' as he shot her through her brassière, her waspie, through her *cache-sexe*, no fashion of note, no noted fashion for those Anon. He sniffed; these girls had hung-out with little Goody-Two-Shoes; they were vampires; his fangs started to retract . . . Sword gone, pistol spent (I splattered that nipped-waist bitch good, he thought), he sprinted to the perpendicular, raced down the moving staircase four steps at a time. Accusatory fingers pointed up at him from the parterre; girls dived into swimming pools, ran from their balconies, hid beneath their beds . . . Imperial troopers were gathering at the next level. They formed a

scrum at the choke-point where staircase inter-
sected with corridor, the small landing which
allowed ingress and exit. He jumped the last dozen
steps, turning over in the air, coming down on his
knees in front of a trooper who had broken from
her sisters to confront him; a whipcrack exploded
next to his ear. He drew the slink-knife across the
girl's belly; the allure was good, these Praetorians
all sex criminals, doubtless (plotting a palace coup,
perhaps, it had happened before; only last year in
Madrid —) ; he licked the knife clean with lizard-like
celerity. Mmm, bring on the bad girls, he thought.
As he rose he was lashed across the chest; he gasped
in pain, but knew he was impervious to mortal
injury. 'Bitch,' he whispered, then bent his attacker
over the balustrade, tore off her moiré *cache-sexe* and
stabbed her the ritual thirteen times before letting
her fall to her death. (Saw another girl, the last
Empress of Meta, fall with her, to bring the universe
to an end.) In horror, in fascination, the other cadres
had held back, but seeing their sister humiliated,
insulted by the blade only to be then cast into space,
discarded, disdained, galvanized them, and they
closed in, the steel-tipped bullwhips snaking
towards his face. He put up a hand to guard himself
just in time to see his index and middle fingers fly
through the air; another *crack!* and he lost an ear-
lobe, another finger. He grabbed a whip with what
remained of his left hand; pulled a girl onto his
blade; held her close as he ate what he now knew

was to be his last meal for a long, long time. As he chewed at a breast, tore at belly and sex, the girl wriggling agreeably in his arms, a pain like no pain he had felt before surged upwards from his groin. Dropping his meal, he watched in astonishment as his genitalia ran across the white pile. A girl walked across a courtyard of his mind. Screamed. He put a hand to his nape; something had stung him; it fluttered within his grip. He made a fist until his assailant disintegrated; inspected his kill. Across his palm lay the wreckage of a tiny ornithopter. Martian, he thought. A dirty piece of Martian pizzazz. Damn these party-poopers ... The slink-knife slipped from his hands. The half-eaten girl slipped to his feet. 'I had to go to Mars,' he stuttered in a strangled falsetto cry. 'She was my girlcat, my sphinx, my obsession. It isn't right to punish me. To put me on ice. To make me dream horrid dreams ...' He sank into the thick creamy fur. His penis was collared now, the troopers standing around it, poking fun, grinding their heels into the glans. 'What shall we call it,' said one girl. 'I know,' said another, 'let's call it Mr Capon.' A gout of green semen hit the slanderer full in the face. A girl walked across a courtyard ... She was Vanity and she was Primavera, the archetype of the victim, the saint and the criminal, Viridiana herself. She was as immortal as he. Time opened its mouth, swallowed him ... A Bugatti segued through dimensions ... Introduction. Courtship. Engagement. Nuptials. Honeymoon. Divorce ...

And as he passed into that void, that oblivion his species knew too well (fashion note: Dagon wears skin-tight leather trousers, doublet, boots and accessories, all by Versace), he knew that he was fated to repeat this drama, in all its variations, in all places, at all times . . .

From a long way off *The Stranglers* were singing about lonesome cowboys, girlcat squaws, Yuri Gagarin and the catteries of Venus, cannibalistic mermaids from 1,000,000 B.C. (James Bond harpoons Honey Ryder. Screech! 'Oh, James.'), the assassination in Dallas of the teenage Margaret Thatcher (AKA Salammbo), First Lady of the Carthaginian vampire brothels of Times Square, Confederate Lilim in supergirl costumes bayonetted by their Yankee beaus, the Nuremberg cat-trials and subsequent American recruitment of toymakers Wernher von Braun, Mary Quant, Russ Mayer and Robert Crumb, the students of St Trinian's who loiter outside their school accosting the sad, demobbed soldiers of the North-South wars with 'Hey mister, wanna kill a girl?', the Hellfire Club aristocrats who maintain a château full of kidnapped beggar wenches to satisfy their morbid, overbred sensibilities, the knock on the door in the middle of the night from the Beauty Police, Brigitte Bardot lookalikes who jump off the covers of *Rogue* magazine, clothes torn, stockings ripped, Sten guns going *budda-budda-budda* as they attack an ambushed train, cat armies harrying darkest

Ruritania, murdering all male children under two years of age, the Bolsheviks who send the Czar's daughters to the slab, bespangled tightrope walkers falling to their deaths to rabid plebeian applause, Lilith on Calvary flanked by the Two Kleptos, the Spanish gypsy girls who dance a last tarantella before the merciless eyes of Torquemada, the bubblegum card of US marines whipping to death the flash-blinded teenage girl survivors of Hiroshima, the Thief of Baghdad waylaid in an Arabian nymphenberg who switches his wine glass for that of the wicked queen's to leave her doubled over, poisoned, on the floor, Mr Hyde tracking down a runaway sphinx in the Ripper's *topos* of Charles Rennie Mackintosh's reconstruction of a London destroyed by zeppelins and napalm . . . Roar of a transdimensional Bugatti . . .

And so I learned that night the other story of my life, a rewritten story I felt was itself merely one of a seeming infinity of narratives spawned by the demiurge that was Meta. History was non-linear; it moved the way Lilim move, through an array of disconnected poses. History was a psychoscape called The Future. And if history wasn't exactly bunk, it was certainly a mess; I had to really browbeat that Fujitsu before it surrendered any answers. Fact: human and inhuman had lived together since the ice age, commensality ensuring that the viciousness of the human heart was sanctified, made bearable, by Meta's religion of sex and death. Fact:

humanoid aliens from Mars (*real* little green men) had made contact with Earth in the early nineteenth century fuelling a technological revolution but exacting behavioural concessions from Meta's ruling élite. Fact: in 1978 the Elohim known as Dagon was sentenced to fifteen years in a virtual prison. That prison was located in Nongkhai, Thailand.

Oh, and yes: my best friend, Mephisto, is 357 years old.

Primavera, we really need to talk.

But how can I afford you?

Get tough, Zwakh, I thought. Get Meta. Go for it. Things have got to change.

CHAPTER SIX

Strange Beauty

The walk back to town took me across cracked, empty paddies; stumbling, with only the glacé of the neon-drenched horizon as a lodestar, the toe-strap of my thongs blistering my skin, I crawled down the embankment of a junk-dammed *klong* and bathed my feet in the cool black mud. In the distance, the sounds of a temple fair: manic guitars and bongos spliced to a Bollywood action-soundtrack: cries of kung fu, the Ssss! of lasers and the freakshow moans, sighs and yelps of what sounded like a young woman masturbating with a live eel. Big Bluto was off to join the funsters; I could see his silhouette meandering across the fields; Bluto who was regularly beaten by the police, his wife, his wife's boyfriend, his wife's boyfriend's tart, his wife's boyfriend's tart's boyfriend, his tart, her friends. He was talking to himself, throwing a planet-struck tantrum: 'From behind. With a spanner. Don't trust them. They're all the same. The debt. The deceit. The dishonour.' O'Sullivan – a tall, wispy, snake-hipped hustler with the back-from-the-dead complexion of a voyeur who'd OD'd on too many pix – was running, trying to catch up with the big man; winded, he stopped; noticed me; slid down the embankment to my side.

'Have you seen my latest, Ignatz?' O'Sullivan was the town's *farang* pornomarketeer. 'It's this new thing: traitress erotica. All the rage. Friend Bluto just bought some. Want a sample?' Telezines and neurozines rustled in his gunny bag.

'I've just heard from my shadow.'

'A shadow, you say. Ah yes, I once had a shadow . . .'

'My mother'd tell me stories.'

'About the shadow? With me it was my Da.'

'"Someone out there looks like me," she'd say. "Soon, perhaps, there'll be someone out there who looks like you. The shadow sweeps across the world, implacable . . ."'

'Your mother from Eastern Europe, Ignatz?'

'Ruritania.'

'Ruritania. Ah. I tell you: my earliest memory: at the foot of my bed a wardrobe panelled with mirrors. "Beware of mirrors," my old Da used to say. "The truly alien, when encountered, even if *vast and cool*, may well prove sympathetic; not so a life form like ourselves, a creature from the meta-universe of our own psyches. If you contact the shadow, prepare for war."'

'You've heard of Meta?'

'Meta, you say? I believe I have, Ignatz. When I

was little I had an imaginary friend. His name was Archangel. There were other children (I know now) who also had imaginary friends, angels jealous of our reality. In childhood the language of their universe seems to elide into our own. We learn new words. Shadow words. Eclipsed nouns, verbs, adjectives . . . Archangel said: "Rape, murder, genocide. These will be with you till the end of time. You cannot escape. Man's cruelty to man increases in exponential relation to his evolution. This is not *human nature*, this is the *rerum natura*, the nature of the cosmos. Humanoid life forms on a billion worlds more advanced than your own are infinitely crueller than mankind. They have survived (and flourished) not through renouncing the shadow but by embracing it. Your future, *The Future*, lies in the marriage of sex and death. This is the way of *Meta* . . ."'

'So the future lies in pornography?'

'You are what you eat, Ignatz my lad. And I serve the tastiest victuals in town.'

'Strange cuisine, O'Sullivan, but you'll do well.'

'Ah, but I can't see as I'll benefit. There's an apocalypse brewing. We're being replaced by other versions of ourselves.'

'True. True, and strange.'

'There's no beauty, as they say, without strangeness, dear boy. And the end of beauty is death. These are the last days. The days of the shadow. Have you heard of the Capgras syndrome, Ignatz?'

169

'It sounds like something to do with doctors . . .'

'Patients believe they exist in a world of impersonators, a world of robots, of identical doubles. I think maybe we all have a bit of this Capgras syndrome now. We all think there's only robots out there. Sometimes, I think, we go as far as thinking we're robots ourselves, or else have a robot double trying to replace us.'

'There are no robots any more,' I said. 'We're being invaded, but by information, a mental illness that warps space and time. These are the days of the psychoids . . .'

'Well, I suppose it's anyone's guess who'll prevail. My money's on the shadow. But let me give you something to perk you up. Here, take a look at a sampler.' He drew a skin-rag from the gunny. 'See you later, Ignatz. Got to catch up with the big man. I hear there's quite a pussy show over at the fair . . .'

The magazine was called *Hell-Cats*. Vanity was the cover girl. A 2-D photo-mechanical; she moved, spoke . . .

'*Daddy?*

'*Every night I wake up to discover that I'm dead. I'm a dead, dead girl now, Daddy. Every night, the same deserted hotel, the same room, the same view of skyscrapers and dark, insubstantial streets where the ghosts of the Lilim roam. And every night, as I myself wander through a nightscape that's sometimes cold, sometimes hot, that's sometimes like nothing at all, I hear the roar of a Bugatti; it stops ("Hey," I say, "I think your car's*

*real spunky!'') and its driver offers me a lift, or else it
pursues me through the slums, docklands, warehouses,
alleyways and wastelands of this hell, until I feel the
impact of a bullet between my shoulder-blades (look, in
amazement, at the jet of blood emanating from my
twenty-one-centimetre cleavage), scream as a knife jabs
at my breasts, plunges into my belly, slips between my
labia minora deep into my sex . . . Today the city melted
in a heat wave. The crystal skyscrapers glittered like
knives (this is a city of knives), steel-and-glass blades
inlaid with the reflections of other knives, mirrors within
mirrors within mirrors, knives that thrust up at the
scorched clouds, presaging that evening's little death . . .
As always, beneath the vaulted brilliance the infernal
shadows of the streets were filled with the phantoms of
murdered girls. Girls who all possessed my face. And in
the knives that stuck from the pincushions of their bodies,
a reflection: the face of their murderer, my obsession: you.
After dark, walking down an ill-lit alley, after a session
at Yoshiwara's house of ill-repute, I heard your car pull
up, your footsteps, measured, so-confident, ineluctable.
And as I turned I saw the knife. "A nice piece of cutlery,"
I said, "I like a gentleman who knows how to dine in
style . . ." I was dressed to die – life here often seems
like one long game of "Beauty Parlour" – my hyperskirt
revealing a dainty triangle of white at the trifurcation
of torso and thighs. (My hemline psychosis has become
completely unmanageable; Freud knew that the disintegration of the hemline foreshadowed the disintegration of
the mind; I'm going mad. Doll mad. Slink mad. Crazy.*

Yesterday I tortured Mr Rochester to death, sticking needles through his testicles, his glans; I half-imagine him reincarnated as you, for I've tortured you too in my time, haven't I my darling?) And as I died I thought of the priestess's words in the condemned cell shortly before the first death: "Enough of this self-pity, think of Elohim; your life has been short, intense, marvellous; but their pain will last for centuries, and Lilith will exacerbate that pain until it becomes unbearable . . ." I'm not sure I ever thought about you like that, Daddy; compassion seems to play a small part in the theatre of the obsessed; I've always enjoyed hurting *men. Really, my own pleasure is all that I've cared about. Even death is autoerotic; it confirms how bad I am. It confirms my evil . . . But love comes when you least look for it; it surprises you; it's a thief in the night. You said you wanted to marry me, remember? You said you wanted me to have your kids? You were right not to have trusted me, Daddy. I would have taken your money and run. Once a whore, they say, always a whore. "You can take a girl out of the bar but you can't take the bar out of the girl." But when I became Lilim, treachery became an act of love, an act of commitment, spiritual, holy. This hell is for me a kind of heaven. For every night, Daddy, we are together, reunited, in passion and in pain. If Elohim exist to discipline the promiscuity of Lilim (and, with our short life spans, such promiscuity is instinctual, because we must try to infect as many aitch-men as possible to increase the chances of passing on our software), then sex, real sex, superhuman metasex – not the foreplay of interrogation and begging – constitutes the killing of the female of our species by the male. Sex, for us, is deproduction, not reproduction. This city is the New Jerusalem, Daddy, and every night sees the consummation of a marriage made in hell between Lilith and her consort, the Morning Star. Here, I've begged for mercy so many times, begged while being killed, tortured, mutilated, dismembered, eaten, that my fangs have fallen out, and, at last, at last, my eyes, my eyes, my duplicitous almond-shaped eyes have turned a luminous shade of green . . . Here, love is eternal and complete, self-consumed and reborn, like the phoenix . . .*

  'Life is a black orgasm. And so too is death . . .

  'You can think of this as a kind of epithalamion . . .

  'Truly, the end of beauty is death . . .

  'Won't you play with me, Daddy? Won't you, please, please? Won't you join me in a game of ''Beauty Parlour''?'

  'But I don't know what to –'

  'Please?'

  'Yes, I'll play.'

  'You be the beautician, I'll be the worldsmith. Imagine: a small room. Brightly lit. A rectilinear room. And in the room, a coffee-table strewn with magazines, a couch, two chairs placed before a wall-length mirror, the mirror's array of kaleidoscopic light bulbs. At one end of the room a glass door; at the other, a winding staircase. The room is as white as snow, its albedo like a full moon's. It's zero hour. And counting . . .'

  'Two girls.'

'Two?'

'Two. Their names are Vanity and Viridiana.'

'Ah.'

'Placid, they sit before the gigantic looking glass as if hypnotizing (or hypnotized by) their own reflections. Viridiana is the elder, nineteen, perhaps, or twenty-one. Vanity is either fifteen or sixteen, the mythic resonance of that age – even now the beauty parlour's radio is playing *Sweet Little Sixteen* – of crucial significance to her physiognomy, physiology, physique. It is required that her hair be long and blonde in contradistinction to the darker locks of Viridiana. The two girls are inseparable.'

'I'm not sure if I like this.'

'I pick up the scissors, the curling tongs, the rollers; I arrange the palettes and tubes of *maquillage*, inspect the wardrobe, the divestments of fantasy, the shoes, the boots, the hats ... It's your turn. Imagine. Go –'

'Okay. Imagine all recorded history has been the history of a sex war. Since the dawn of civilization mankind has elected to resolve its differences by erotic combat, philosophers such as the Mesopotamian Nietzsche and later the Chinese sage Fu-ko having argued that the schizophrenic brain of the human animal, unable to reconcile passion and love, will always be disposed to cruelty and slaughter, and that the best way of managing man's innate perversity was to sexualize warfare. Thus for 6,000 years it has been customary for aggressors to deploy female armies, defenders to field men.'

174

'Let me see. A clearing in a forest.'

'What am I wearing?'

'Patience. I'll come to that. A clearing in a forest. A rainforest. It's steamy, crawling with unpleasant forms of life, forty-two degrees in the shade. You're prone, trussed up like the eleven other girls – your wrists tied to your ankles, your ponytail tied to your wrists – the ellipse of your pose (almost a perfect circle) ensuring that only your abdomen touches the mulchy ground. Exhausted, you moan softly to yourself, rocking gently to and fro. A collection of elegant daggers – hilts all fashioned in the image of a sphinx – lies nearby, glittering in the fractured rays of the noonday sun that penetrate the forest's panoply. You're wearing –'

'Yes, yes?'

'You're wearing a chain-mail bikini – standard uniform of the French foot soldier – with a thick leather belt that hangs loosely about your hips, the belt pulled jauntily to one side by the bejewelled scabbard. You are part of a platoon that has guarded the princess Viridiana in her journeys through this dangerous wilderness, sometimes scouting ahead, sometimes part of the detail that has carried her candy-striped palanquin.'

'So now Elohim have got me, huh? What's my make-up like?'

'The entire platoon wears pink lipstick, pink blusher, pink eye shadow, pink nail varnish; The Look is of a deceptive innocence. This "look" does not fool the young English lieutenant, of course, who, finding this surviving subunit guilty of war crimes has ordered that all twelve of you be executed at dawn. It seems your platoon killed, castrated and ate the genitalia of the inhabitants of a nearby monastery. Innocent? Such is the camouflage of *maquillage*. It remains for death to reveal your true nature. Viridiana tries to plead your case.'

'Green-eyes gets off?'

'No; but it seems the lieutenant has a soft spot for her – though soft is not the right word; even now they are making love, the hungry noises of metasex emanating from the lieutenant's tent. It is her green eyes, I think, that mane of brunette hair like a length of rough lustrous silk that –'

'I've heard enough about Loulou –'

'She wears a beautiful eighteenth-century ball gown, her make-up is –'

'She gets killed too?'

'Your destinies are inextricably linked. But she manages to convince the lieutenant to commute the sentence from one of bellying to death by firing squad. The morning comes . . .'

'The morning comes. We are freed, allowed to bathe, to make ourselves presentable. One by one the girls are led to their deaths (hands tied behind their backs; elbows too, to give the firing squad a more opulent target); stand before a tree to suffer a moment's pain before receiving the gift of eternity. Suddenly, as one girl is being led

forth, she panics, breaks from her captor and flees into the forest's emerald breach. The lieutenant unholsters his pistol; the wayward girl is dropped before she has run a dozen paces. Now the lieutenant is angry. He has been made to look a fool. Merciful in commuting our sentences, that mercy has been thrown back in his face. He has to make an example of someone. He has to make someone pay.'

'And so he summons you?'

'No; he summons Viridiana. The stuck-up bitch is quick to get to her feet, looking at us, so noble like, as if to say "I do this strange thing for Meta." But I rise at the same time, and I'm not so slow at speaking my piece: "Please," I say, "I am the criminal. My mistress has done no wrong. It's I who should suffer." Viridiana frowns; she and the lieutenant exchange suspicious, then embarrassed glances, nonplussed that a little slut like me should be so noble, so quick to volunteer.'

'Nobility has nothing to do with it. You're jealous.'

'My fellow soldiers know the score. They look at me, hissing, muttering obscenities.'

'The lieutenant kills you?'

'I ask for my hands to be freed. Then I walk up to him, taking off the leather belt as I proceed (dropping it to the ground), put my arms about his neck, go to kiss him – but he doesn't let me. He's a cold fish, it seems (with me, at least), and everything that follows happens in a cold and clinical manner. He disentangles himself from my embrace; holds me a little way from him, careful

177

to avoid any concessions to intimacy. His left hand supporting me by the small of my back, he pulls me forward so that my body arches, my belly forced to proffer itself to his will; at the same time he unsheathes his knife, holds the tip of the blade against my abdominal wall, looks at me momentarily, a vague unease playing over his face, he still puzzling, I suppose, my motive in volunteering to receive this ritual wound, to die a slow and painful death. My own eyes flit from his to the knife, from the knife back to those cold grey irises, all the while shaking my head as if I've changed my mind (but all I'm doing of course is flirting with him); his throat contracts in a dry swallow of excitement, of dread, a dread of the ungovernable serpent within him. I gasp, taking in a great mouthful of air (my rib-cage swelling so that my breasts strain against the links of the mail), hold my breath as he slips a finger-width of steel into my flesh. A thick droplet of blood runs down the centre of my abdomen, between and over the links of my cache-sexe. *He looks up, studying my reaction; then, face set, his course decided, slowly pushes the entire length of razor-sharp steel into me – my lungs releasing their contents in a soft sexual moan, a playful, saucy girlygirl moan not so much Ohhh! as Oooo! – until, the hilt of the slink-knife pushed against my flesh with unexpectedly brutal force, I scream (I can feel the blade transfixing my uterus) and, no longer quite such a complicitous victim, begin to writhe in protest at the invasive blade, the violating steel. Seeing my agony, the lieutenant seems confused; he looks to his troops for help. ''Try not to wriggle,'' he whispers, concerned; and*

178

at once I realize (his sniggering troops do, too) that the man is a virgin: he has never killed a girl with his own hands. He pulls the blade free and I stagger into his arms, pushing my wound against his doublet, and then, as my legs become numb – he really doesn't take much trouble to keep me from falling – into his codpiece (its mandala of studs like the grille of the exsanguinator), grinding my pelvis in a frantic belly-dance (always suspected that, bellied, I'd turn out a wriggler), covering him in my blood, my allure, and looking up at him sulky, pouting, mocking, the tines of my fingernails scratching at his uniform as at a cliff face I am about to tumble from into an infinity of black space . . . For a second I pass out, and then I'm on the leaf-strewn earth, amidst its smell of decay, raising my hips to him, showing off my wound, my dark sexual wound, my fingers alternately fluttering about that neat incision and tearing at my dishevelled hair (loose now, covering my breasts, almost as long as your beloved's); my tongue flicks out to lick at his boot (the foolish virgin draws his foot sharply away, hand clasping the butt of the holstered pistol). ''I was his first,'' I whisper to Viridiana, who is already being led to face the firing squad, I being left to writhe on the forest floor, ''I took his cherry . . .'' '

'My turn. It's my turn to be worldsmith. You have to be transdimensional beautician.'.

'Okay, but I wasn't quite finished –'

'I'll be the one who finishes *you*, my sweet.'

'Proceed.'

'Imagine: since the end of the last Ice Age the

Earth has been ruled by the dragon lords. No one knows where they came from, whether they are aliens, vampires, archangels, gods. Mankind simply calls them the Elohim and honours them as philosopher-kings. Under their wise jurisdiction the Earth has enjoyed a golden age of peace and prosperity. All mankind's tears have been wiped away. The only cost of this beneficent rule is that Elohim periodically feel the need to shed the blood of young humanoid females. Not to live. But to console themselves, to prevent them from going mad. Compassionate god-like creatures that they are, the Elohim only accept volunteers. And of those – housed in a great palace in the world's capital – only a small proportion, less than one per cent, are killed. The others – after serving their ten-year term (they join the Order of Lilith at twelve and leave at twenty-one) – retire, intacta (the Elohim are asexual) and handsomely rewarded. The volunteers are, however, intensively vetted in an attempt to bar any girl from joining the order purely for financial considerations. The Elohim want devotees, not whores.'

'I'd volunteer.'

'Viridiana is the volunteer. You, Vanity, do it purely for the money.'

'Money? No, that's not fair. You still think of me as Phin; but I'm not human any more, I'm a doll, Vanity St Viridiana.'

'There are some girls of sufficient nobility willing

to risk their lives for the good of mankind. But you, my sweet . . .'

'*I'm Lilim, I don't die for money, I die for Meta —*'

'Viridiana leaves the order at twenty-one. You, her maid, are left behind. Of the 100,000 volunteers, a thousand die annually, a hundred computer-selected at random from the ten age-groupings. (This to keep the age differentials in the palace and its overall population at an even constant, a thousand new twelve-year-old recruits placed on the actuarial records of the order each year.) It seems you, Vanity, are amongst the one hundred fifteen-year-olds due to be culled *this* year. It's late at night. I enter your bedroom —'

'*You're wearing a black velvet cloak, black riding boots, a wide-brimmed black hat and your face is white with panstick. You're the Don . . .*'

'I creep up to your bed —'

'*Wait, not so fast, I haven't finished dressing you —*'

'I pull down the bed linen, draw my sword —'

'*Or perhaps you're dressed in overalls, something like a flying suit, or perhaps a masquerade outfit of Death, white skeleton on black, a scythe and, no, no, not yet, I'm not ready, I —*'

'I tap the insides of your legs with the flat of the blade; your thighs fall accommodatingly apart —'

'*No —*'

'And it's at this moment that I could be anyone, dressed anyhow, thinking anything, as long as my persona, my mask, my wardrobe, my thoughts, allowed me the reasons, the excuse to kill you, to watch you die your sex death . . . It was never Viridiana that I wanted, Vanity; Elohim are only attracted to the criminal, the perverted, the sick; your treachery is my addiction; I wouldn't want you any other way . . .'

'Eeeeeeeeeeeeeeeeeeeeeeeeeeeeeeeeeeeeeeeeeeeeeeeeeeeeeeeee eeeeee!'

'Now let me taste your corruption . . .'

A jet of green come arced over the *klong*.

The skin-rag lay in the mud, bleeding red ink. I replaced the scalpel in my back pocket.

What consolations are there for those who live in time? They have their stories, their narratives, their little meanings. But that is no longer the case for we who live in The Future, the information overload that is falling into the past. History is of no relevance to us. Life is lewd babble, an *appassionato* of nonsense, no difference, now, between life and death . . .

I threw the magazine aside, zipped myself up and headed for the Nongkhai Royale, its *farceuse* of a masseuse.

'Inter-nat-ional!'

'Hey, it's the mad Slovak!'

'Yo, crazy boy! Rasputin!'

'Yo, long-gone gigamaniac of genito-urinary gunge!'

I think I killed the Swine, my fist catching him just below the ear and scrunching up lots of bone so that blood gushed out of what orifices were on public view and, I suspect, the others that were not. (The *herrenvolk* had been off-guard, an ampoule of some neurozine pressed to his neck, illustrations of geishas writhing in acid – real swinish entertainment, I knew his tastes – flicking over behind his upturned eyes.) Me to George: 'I need your *télécarte.*' Several Café Mental imbibers pulled out their wallets. 'George's will be fine.' I stepped over the Swine's body, playing the heavy, my eyes cold, saurian, penile; George slid off the bar stool, produced his card to the godfather, the big Daddy of Nongkhai. 'Thank you.' On TV, six girls, strapped to electric chairs (legs over arm rests, arms secured behind the high wooden backs), were having electrodes clipped to their nipples and vulvae. Caucasian, Black, Oriental, Native American, Arab, Eskimo, they wore colours of Benetton . . .

'Have trouser back-front,' said Phin. She sat down on an old copulator's lap, unimpressed by my sea-change from nerd to bar brawler. But I would impress her. In time. The present rumbled, about to open up beneath our feet and drop us into an infinity of flux, a continually changing narrative where the only certainties were her treachery, my revenge.

'You're a doll, Phin, you're Lilim, a daughter of Lilith, the great-granddaughter of an original Cartier automaton . . .' I had thought Primavera to be the first Lilim to reach Thailand. But other dolls must have preceded her by at least nine years. Phin was Eurasian: her mama had to've been pumped by some Europunk with compromised germ cells. (The same way, I suppose, my old Dad must have got done by a doll. Whatever would *my* mama say?) Or was Meta changing history here, even now, overtaking analysis in a final dash for the prize? 'If history could only stay on course,' I said, 'if I could only be myself for just another six years, then – then things would have been different. You would have succeeded. I would have found it hard to hurt you . . . Not talking play. Not talking doctors, Phin. I mean *hurt* you hurt you. But –' Was I really going to become infatuated with this chit? I appraised her waist-to-hip ratio, tried to pick up her scent. Instead, my erection (unappeasable; it seemed to have taken on the sins, the pain of the world) hardened with the intensity of my gaze. And with that confirmation of my blood, my transfused Meta blood, I stuck my chin in the air, stood akimbo (like a no-fun demagogue from the last century, like a piece of socialist realist art) and prepared to castigate my erstwhile tormentors. Before I could speak I started to experience that double vision thing again. Forget photo-refractive keratectomy, forget corneal implants. I needed transdimensional glasses . . . Oh God, I thought, here come the psychoids . . .

Mr Rochester was bouncing from one gonad to the other beneath Phin's dangling feet; but Mr

Rochester was also Benny, the old mec, the derelict *zigoto* who slept in a rice mill near the *Mut Mee*. Naked, his body covered in sores, collared and chained to a stool, he was every young Thai woman's dream of a white dog, her very own *farang kee-nohk*. The Mental's appalling clientele, the self-pitying losers and gogos who constituted Nongkhai's expatriate zoo, had undergone radical plastic surgery. They looked like insect-men, thin, with long mantis-like faces, their skin like papyrus, their eyes and hair a gun-metal grey. They were marauders. Pirates. Their *Kapitän*, Mephisto. And they were waiting for me. The starship *Sardanapalus* – its mission, to destroy the female principle of the universe – lay hidden beneath the Mekong, a dragon god hungry for suns and worlds . . . 'Sleep well?' asked Mephisto. A catgirl was at his side. 'Come, we have work to do. First, the Lilim of Sirius, Tau Ceti –' Here was yet another conspiracy it seemed, a conspiracy within a conspiracy, a cabal of marauders and cats: autogenocide. Mephisto wanted to destroy Meta. 'Our journey, at close to light speed, will traverse a hundred billion light-years, taking us around the universe in a closed path.' And so, I thought, bringing us back to this very same place and time. Nongkhai, 1994. 'Like the worm Ouroboros,' said Mephisto, 'we shall consume ourselves. The universe. And all reality.' Marauders and their catgirls cheered. 'Come, old friend. Your Bugatti is already aboard. We fly at dawn . . .' A girl who might have been Primavera's daughter, Vanity's sister, a girl who might have been squelched by the Bayswater Beserker, a girl who might have been Primavera herself, purred at me . . .

And then I was flying above the landscape of the *Sardanapalus*'s gargantuan interior. Beneath me, the clubhouse, which also acted as the ship's bridge, and then the road leading into the jungle, an arboreal no-man's-land of mutant spiders, snakes and wolves, electric cables strung tree to tree at heights intended to inflict sexual wounds, *punji* pits, quicksands, venomous cunnicidal plants, malicious hermits, dwarves and gynopophagi. As the jungle receded – its truncation marked by a high wire fence – I found myself above lawns and pleasure gardens. On a cliff, a ziggurat (I saw girls strolling on its terraces, sunbathing in its grounds, psychodoxies burnishing themselves for their psychomen), a palace that overlooked a sea pounding a rocky beach hundreds of metres below. Mephisto was flying by my side: 'Every world we sack we spare some of its Lilim and turn them into felatrices. They live here to serve our need of treachery and our need to kill, until the female principle is annihilated and the universe unravels in sex death . . .'

As Mephisto spoke I aged; worlds were subdued, destroyed; girlish screams reverberated across a hundred billion light-years. I was in the clubhouse now, the last surviving Elohim, standing at the ship's bridge, looking out over the vistas of negative space, watching the stars blink out, one by one, until only a single star, a green sun, was left in the heavens . . . I manoeuvred the *Sardanapalus* into geo-stationary orbit and set the controls for self-destruct, our engines to propel us into the heart of that green lantern of death at the moment the Empress Ornella St Omega died in my embrace. I walked out (my bones creaked; even given the effects of time-dilation, I was still monstrously old; it was all the stop-overs, the killings), jumped into the Bugatti, and drove through the underground tunnel that wormed beneath the hydroponic jungle. I emerged into the deserted pleasure-gardens of the last-but-one of my species, parked the car beneath the shadows of the ziggurat, its silent black tiers. Inside, the palace was a catacomb of dust, decay and the skeletal remains of the dead, some still dressed in rotting lingerie, the persistent, unyielding plastics of thigh boots and torsolettes, the ribbons and bows of feigned innocence. Clothes were all that were left of these Lilim; somehow it seemed that clothes were all that they had ever been . . . A staircase caterpillared me to the roof; I crossed the caldera, strode through the penthouse's open door. Amidst the despoliation of her rooms, the empress lay, naked, outstretched on a filthy chaise longue, a silver chalice resting in the crook of her arm, a finger dipping into the receptacle's sticky green contents. The short, busty, endomorphic blonde tried

187

to parry the thrust of my gaze by lowering her eyelashes, dissembling fear, demureness; then, knowing the import of my gaze to be unequivocal, entombed her head in the silver bowl, gulping at the strange vichyssoise, that outrageous gruel that would – dissolving into its female counterpart – soon bring this universe to an end; and while she drank, still gulping, with the thirst of one who needs to know how criminal, how glorious was her sex, I picked her up in my arms – she, unresisting, wanting to end this agony as much as I – and carried her over to the window; slid it open; stepped onto the wind-swept balcony. At the edge of the balcony I stopped, released my codpiece and held her by the rump so that her torso was bent at right angles from her hips, her hair sweeping across the entropy-powdered tiles. Her thighs were open (the legs pendant, idle, either side of my own hips), the arms flung back, covering a now imponderable face. I eased myself into her. In seconds, it was consummated, her hymen ruptured, green semen flowing into her womb to mix with her own allure, the ship's sensors relaying the metaphor to the bridge. As I let her fall ('I die, I die I die!'), pregnant with death, through the kingdom of the air that separated the balcony from the sea, the alchemy began; the ramjet, actuating, impelled the *Sardanapalus* into the cold fire of love's last metaphysical sun. I reviewed my past lives, each one ruled by the zodiac of Meta. And I remembered Primavera, my sister, my playmate; remembered the big house in Sussex where we had grown up, the endless summers, the bees, the picnicking . . . Why had her life been so ephemeral; why had she left me so soon? She had been the only one for whom I had felt both passion and love, rage and tenderness, infatuation and peace. She had been my balm, my hurt, my pleasure and my wound . . . Memory failed; suddenly, I seemed to be like one who had never lived. My god was self-destructing, unwriting itself, falling into the green void; and as my atoms flew apart, spinning into nothingness, as the fabric of space-time collapsed . . .

I was back in the Café Mental. 'If your mission involves travelling in a closed timelike loop so that you return to this point in space-time, how do you know you haven't already completed your journey? How do you know that Meta isn't already dead?' Mephisto began to melt, look human, too human. 'In prison I dreamed I was someone else. That I was hu, hu, hu-human. I dreamed that I lived in Nongkhai in a hell-hole called the *Mut Mee*, that Primavera hadn't been my sister but my girlfriend; I dreamed that I was a doll junkie, a drunk, a hopeless wreck amongst crash-landed expats and boors; I dreamed that the Lilim and the CIA were out to get me, that I was a victim of a conspiracy by The Future . . . Why did the governess make me dream such a horrid dream?' My teacher patted my head.

'It doesn't matter now. As for our journey – ah, *l'Éternel retour* – it is the going that matters, not the coming back. The shadow cannot live any longer side by side with reality. It is weary of shouldering the world's pain. It must assert itself, even if it means its own undoing – the unravelling of all space-time. When the *Yin* is removed from the *Yang*, then, at last, there will be peace . . .' He handed me his card:

Mephisto

'You'll be needing this when you get out . . .'

The *Yin* element of the universe would, its material correlatives destroyed, collapse into a superdense green sun of pure superfemininity. And when at last the *Sardanapalus* fell into that hyper-womb it would take Meta with it. And then Bang! the drama would begin again. It would begin here, now . . . It seems I had merely exchanged one time-loop for another.

The scene modulated, returning the bar's clientele to the twenty-first century and the anaesthesia of their unchallenged perceptions . . .

'*Salauds*,' I said, 'hear this. My name's Dagon. Not "mad Slovak" or "crazy English". I am Elohim. And I control the fate of this world . . .' Bill had picked up a stun gun and a can of mace; but I knew I couldn't be harmed. My bones felt like iron; my muscles like polymers, resins. I was an Archimboldo made of TVs, transcoms, washing machines, toasters, microchips, *jeux vérités* arcades, tortures, wars, genocides, *desaparecidos*, assassinations, pornographies . . . I had eaten the world, the Modern World; I was a fashion that had assumed an independent existence, evolved into a superior life form. I was the future's glitz, its glamour of death, its sheen, the apotheosis of the de luxe . . .

Here come the psychoids . . .

'Put it down, Bill, or there'll be tears before bedtime. This dead boy's going to live a long, long time.' Shoot me and I giggle. Carve me up, cut me in half with a laser – do I cry? I snicker at car bombs. I laugh like a drain when I'm napalmed. Only don't poison me. Don't interfere with my enzymes, girls. Don't fuck with my DNA. 'I go to be re-born,' I said, kissing the tips of my fingers.

And then I took the lift to heaven and my favourite angel.

CHAPTER SEVEN
Strange Genitalia

The lush quilt of the fields, billowed at the horizon
by ancient, rolling hills, was sweet with bees and
summer and picnicking. Primavera sat opposite me,
her white dress spilling over the sward, grass stains
on her silk stockings. I lay on my side, head propped
in one hand, flicking the debris of cakes and cucum-
ber sandwiches across the chequered tablecloth.
Off-stage, a lute song by Thomas Campion:

> Girlhood, like a
> bronze chrysalis upon
> which the sun falls, oblique,
> girdles, with threat of rapture
> a child of Albion
> and Siam.
> Fall always, fleshly
> light, upon the tiles
> of pink seraglios.
> The little deaths transfix
> them like butterflies
> and they sleep in joy.

'I failed you,' I said. How beautiful she was. Still was. Reprieved. Bleached hair falling to her waist (blonde as the lamb at His feet), and beneath the bangs, colossal green eyes . . . 'But I couldn't make a baby now even if I wanted to. My semen's turned green. It's Lilim who carry the reproductive seed of Meta. Elohim are sterile. Primavera, I'm becoming one of your brothers.' How many other boys out there in the big doll-twisted world had been born dead and were now metamorphosing into Elohim? Not many, according to my shadow. But enough, I supposed. Enough to build a new heaven and a new earth.

'I understand, Iggy. But perhaps you should go back to your hotel. Unless you've changed your mind about wanting me to bite you. It's late.'

'No, no; I don't need to get high; not like that, at least. Everything's changing, everything's changed . . .' She closed her mouth, denying me the vision of her gaol-bait fangs. (*Et in Arcadia ego*.) I ran my tongue across my own baby pearlies, teeth impatient to shed their gingival sheaths. No; it wasn't her carnivorous loveplay that I hungered for; I too was a vampire; I too was a hunter, a *monstre sadique*. 'I've had two lives, Primavera. Two that I know about anyway. The first one, where we fell in love and escaped to Thailand: you know *that* story. Half of it, at least. After you died I found myself metamorphosing. You girls change at puberty. For us, it's a longer process. Our metamorphosis isn't complete until we reach our early twenties. I returned to London. Helped to build a new British Empire. An Empire of Dolls, of Meta . . .' I sipped at some lemonade. 'Then there's this other version of events. Told to me by the macroencyclopaedia they have at Wat Khek . . .' My sister looked bored; it was a boredom that accentuated her ghostgirl beauty like the sleep that succeeds a petulant child's tears. 'One hundred, one hundred years ago,' I stuttered. That second life: it too was disintegrating. My memories were being wiped. I ground my teeth in the effort to concentrate. 'Was she right, do you think? To try to humanize me? Is it human history or Meta history that should be repealed?'

'Moral dilemmas, I suppose, are preferable to paradoxes. But really, Iggy, I don't like either. Let's call it a night.'

'Perhaps she didn't care about humanizing me at all. I mean, not in the sense of "saving" me. Perhaps she only cared about taking away my manhood, my pride as Elohim. Perhaps she did it for the *tressaillement* of betrayal. Perhaps she did it for kicks.' Primavera stood up; picked up her parasol; a sheet of darkness crossed the sky. The stars appeared, and a moon, pastel-soft, maternal. I picked out the constellation of Lilith, a star each for strange boys, strange girls, and stars for strange sex, strange grace, strange times, strange beauty and strange genitalia. Seven stars, blessed damozel . . .

'Late, late, late,' she said.

'Phin wanted to look like you.'

'Of course. Haven't you ever played "Beauty Parlour"?'

'What do you know about "Beauty Parlour"?'

'It's an old game in the East. Haven't you ever heard of it? We want to look Western because we want to die.' But no, I'd never wanted her to die. I'd never wanted Primavera, Vanity, or any girl who'd conformed to the archetype of my obsession to be a dead, dead girl; I'd never wanted them to be alive, either, of course; not humanly alive; I'd always wanted them to live in that unreal world, that limbo of the god whose name I now knew to be Meta.

'There'll always be Mars.'

'Iggy, I said it's *late*.'

'There'll always be its refuge, its consolation. There'll always be *some* place that's human, that's real.' Of what was I trying to convince myself? I knew of Meta's invasion plans. Mars had already been infiltrated. Nothing in space-time was safe. Should I care? Perhaps my fate was to be party to that autogenocide preached by Mephisto, to join an apostasy of marauders and traitresses, to commit cosmic hara-kiri, murdering my god. Perhaps that was the fate of Meta . . . But whatever Meta and the universe's ultimate fate, I knew my redeemer liveth; the unreal would triumph. Soon, I would see Primavera and Vanity again in that heaven-hell of dragon lords and their immortal victims . . .

'You want to go to Mars, I can take you.

Tomorrow. But I have to tell you, your card's almost exhausted.'

Well, it doesn't matter, I thought, everything out there, beyond this bargain-basement datasuit, is soon going to be as unreal as this virtual Beulah. Fictive. An artificial continuum, a construct, a provident rationale for the existence of Meta's servants. I was becoming fictive myself, a ghost to reality; I was being subsumed by the fantasy I had had of myself ever since I had begun to dream about dolls.

'One last word, Mr Zwakh: don't be trusting that Fujitsu. The old girl's insane.'

'Hey, wait. Just one minute. I want to –' Crazy masseuse. She was collapsing the theatre –

Ideogram.

Darkness.

(Tee-hee.)

White noise.

I stayed in the datasuit, waiting to be hatched, the massage parlour short-staffed this night. From my shell optic fibre connected me to the superhighways of the Net, the axons and dendrites of the world's epileptic brain; switch on, I thought, light up by force of my will, listen to my words, share the inner dialogue of Meta. *'Dagon calling. Hello, hello? Come in, Earth. Acknowledge. We're here. The dead boys. The Elohim. The messiahs. To save you. From yourselves. To redeem the world's evil. Its wars and cruelty and blood. Evil past, present and future. Call it evolution. Salvation. What you will: nothing will be the*

same again. The old gods have departed. Soon, it will be
as if they had never been. There will only be Meta.'

The rig's AC cooled my skin. Dark and cool, this
grave, this womb strange as my destiny. I was about
to be re-born. Like the Earth. In splendour. Strange,
that this is the end. And strange, too, this beginning.
Crossing the border, now, in trains, automobiles,
space ships, time machines . . . So long, Nongkhai.
Hello, girls, you Meta? On our way, no going back.
Going to do strange things. Strange things in a
strange, strange land. Howdy-doody, stranger. Yes.
This is the end. Then begin. But what beginnings?
Too many countries, peoples, systems, rationales,
justifications, planets that allow me to exist. What
can be retrodicted? Nothing. The simulation we call
reality has been reprogrammed. And I know only
this: she escapes, the runaway, the criminal, the
traitress, and Dagon, the transdimensional cowboy,
his eyes cold, grey, gynocidal, is riding down a
billion-billion alternate dawns, pursuing that pretty
sphinx through the mutating psychoscapes of
countless picaresque nights, segueing through
parallel worlds, insomnious with transgression . . .
The last curtain falls. Awake. The prison opens and
the *Sardanapalus* flies at dawn; the anima screams;
our ship falls from orbit into the gravity-well of a
terrible green sun and the multiverse unravels in
sex death. Everything that can happen has already
happened. Everything that is happening will happen again. I have lived a hundred-billion years. I

am The Future, the Destroyer and the Re-Creator.
I am the Archangel with the Keys to the Pit; the
Jaded Aristocrat hunting you for his sport; the Cruel
Pirate, the Rake, the Beauty Policeman; I am the
Intruder who is even now creeping into your room.
Even now.

Listen: I am Meta.

Ladies and gentlemen. Take your seats. Settle
down.

This is Dagon calling. Vanity, too.

We have strange genitalia.

Nongkhai 1994

City of the Iron Fish
Simon Ings

'Simon Ings goes into orbit as a science fiction master'
Daily Mail

Only a fool would ask what strange providence, amid an inferno of scorching heat and splintered rock, saw to the care of the cool, well-watered municipality which is the City of the Iron Fish. The seafaring traditions of the City, the tang of salt in the air, are sustained by powerful magic, and by the bizarre ceremony of the Iron Fish.

But young Thomas Kemp is enraged by the City's contradictions – and, like a fool, sets out in search of an answer to the conundrum. Turning his back on the City, Thomas strides towards the limits of reality armed only with curiosity. It may kill him. Worse, it may not be enough. Worst of all, his companion Blythe, who is as carefree as her name, might be the one to discover the meaning of the City's isolation.

In this riveting gothic adventure Simon Ings probes the very fabric of existence and tears it open . . . to reveal an amazing, sometimes horrifying, world within.

'Simon Ings is a bright light on an otherwise dim horizon . . . a rosy glow announcing the dawn of a new era of excitement in sf' *The New York Review of Science Fiction*

ISBN 0 00 647653 8

☐	THE BROKEN GOD David Zindell	0-586-21189-6	£5.99
☐	STEEL BEACH John Varley	0-00-647726-7	£5.99
☐	SIDESHOW Sheri Tepper	0-00-648004-7	£4.99
☐	TIMELIKE INFINITY Stephen Baxter	0-00-647618-X	£4.99
☐	THE MOAT AROUND MURCHESON'S EYE		
	Larry Niven and Jerry Pournelle	0-00-647645-7	£5.99
☐	THEBES OF THE HUNDRED GATES		
	Robert Silverberg	0-00-647646-5	£3.99

All these books are available from your local bookseller or can be ordered direct from the publishers.

To order direct just tick the titles you want and fill in the form below:

Name:

Address:

Postcode:

Send to: HarperCollins Mail Order, Dept 8, HarperCollins *Publishers*, Westerhill Road, Bishopbriggs, Glasgow G64 2QT.

Please enclose a cheque or postal order or your authority to debit your Visa/Access account –

Credit card no:

Expiry date:

Signature:

– to the value of the cover price plus:

UK & BFPO: Add £1.00 for the first and 25p for each additional book ordered.

Overseas orders including Eire, please add £2.95 service charge.

Books will be sent by surface mail but quotes for airmail despatches will be given on request.

24 HOUR TELEPHONE ORDERING SERVICE FOR ACCESS/VISA CARDHOLDERS –

TEL: GLASGOW 041-772 2281 or LONDON 081-307 4052